MW00911677

WINNER OF THE
32ND ANNUAL
INTERNATIONAL
3-DAY NOVEL
CONTEST

2808
928 Homer St
B6Z2 5233

SNOWMEN

MARK
SEDORE

3-Day Books
Vancouver · Toronto

Cover and interior design by Mauve Pagé.
Cover photo by iStockphoto/
  Ryerson Clark.
Printed in Canada by Friesens.

LIBRARY AND ARCHIVES CANADA
CATALOGUING IN PUBLICATION

Sedore, Mark, 1979-
  Snowmen / Mark Sedore.

ISBN 978-1-55152-366-8

  I. Title.

PS8637.E43S66 2010
  C813'.6   C2010-903792-8

Distributed in Canada by University of
Toronto Press and in the United States by
Consortium through Arsenal Pulp Press
(www.arsenalpulp.com).

This is a work of fiction. Any resemblance
to persons either living or deceased is
purely coincidental.

PUBLISHED BY:
3-Day Books
PO Box 2106, Station Terminal
Vancouver, BC V6B 3T5 Canada
E: info@3daynovel.com
W: www.3daynovel.com

Mixed Sources
Cert no. SW-COC-001271
© 1996 FSC
FSC

To my parents,
Clare and Dolores

O N E

I PUT MY HAND TO MY LIPS AND PRESS WARMTH INTO THE back of my thumb until I can feel it again. I thought it was just a small tear in the right-hand glove and that I could get by just fine without repairing it. And even now, though I have to stop every five minutes and feed warmth into it, maybe it's nothing I should be too worried about this early in the journey. Who knew my knife was so sharp?

In eighteenth-century Iceland they wouldn't have had this problem. Centuries ago the fishermen there realized that the thumb part of the glove was the first to wear out. You'd use the crook of your thumb to haul in the line, to rig the sail or push the oar, depending on the type of boat. You'd hold the hooks of the nets on your thumb and toss them out into the water with a flick of your wrist. If, Odin forbid, you fell into the North Atlantic, a strong grip on the side of the boat was your only hope of survival. If you didn't have your thumbs warm and free for that, you were lost. So the fishermen insisted on two thumbs on each pair of gloves. They were reversible. When the one got worn out, you'd just flip it over and you'd have another thumb to keep your flesh from freezing while you haul your line or cast your nets.

Me, I'm not so lucky.

I look at the tear in the fabric. The tape I've been using to cover it up has come off again. The triple-layered fibre of the glove should have been impossible to damage but my knife was sharper than my glove was strong. I'm lucky I didn't slice my skin open.

I stop in the middle of a small, frozen lake and start undoing the complicated harness system that secures my pack to my outerwear. I have three different types of tape with me in accordance with the inventory my brother laid out. All the tape is suitable for sub-zero temperatures. If I don't run out, they should serve to hold my glove together for the next...but I don't want to think about that. The pack lands on the ice with a disappointing silence. For all its weight and density it is remarkably padded and comfortable. I roll my shoulders with the freedom of one having just escaped from prison and my thumb aches from the cold leaking through the tear. I take off my goggles and squint as I search through the pack—the goggles are great for reducing snow glare, but pretty much useless for doing any real work. I grab the first roll of tape I come to, bright pink, and re-wrap my thumb mummy-style until the Arctic air can't find any more cracks to steal my heat. There's probably a better way to do it, but I'm damned if I can remember anything about emergency equipment patches from the three-day winter survival course I took back in Ottawa. Only a few short weeks ago, of course, but it may as well be a century.

I haven't eaten anything for a few hours, so while I'm in the pack I pull out an energy bar. It's my second-last one, but I'm only a couple of kilometres from the next food cache. I stand up and look at the bright landscape around me. I knew the Canadian Arctic was going to be white, but this was *really* white. It's still mid-June, so the sun doesn't ever sink fully below the horizon, though neither does it rise terribly high above it. All the shadows are long and, at this time of day, pointed in the direction I'm headed: straight north. The shadows of the white crags, the white rocks. Even my breath casts a long white shadow on the white ground.

I look back at where I've come from and see that my footprints leave barely perceptible white indentations behind me. Little marks of my passage filled with just a slightly darker shade of white than everything else.

I hoist the pack again, do up the buckles and start trekking in the direction of the food cache.

Walking, I wonder vaguely what day it is. Probably Thursday. Maybe Wednesday. A few days ago I'd turned off the time and date function on the GPS. Knowing where I was on the planet and how far I was travelling was good enough for me. In a land of perpetual light, knowing that it was eleven o'clock at night was only discouraging. I've adopted a sleep-when-I'm-tired, eat-when-I'm-hungry routine.

If it is Wednesday, Sandra might be making some kind of pasta after her yoga class right now, before sitting down to watch the evening news without me. Thinking of Sandra's cooking makes me realize how hungry I am; energy bars are good for keeping you going, but they are *awful* for filling your stomach.

Where's the food cache? My GPS says I should be right on top of it. Since I'm the only thing in the entire landscape with colour—a garish mixture of black and yellow outerwear, green headgear, orange backpack and, of course, bright-pink thumb—the black, metallic cache should be easy to spot. Sometimes they land in crevasses, though. Sometimes the Arctic wind has covered them in snow particles. Sometimes when they land they're still warm from the plane and if there's any condensation in the air—extremely rare in this desert climate—they'll accumulate a thick coating of frost, making them almost invisible. With the boxes being dropped from a hundred metres up I wonder if the occasional one would explode on impact, but so far the ones I've come across have been intact. I turn up the brightness on the GPS and, while staring intently at it to make sure I'm not reading it wrong, I trip over something solid and hard and I fall, landing heavily on my chest.

I am an extremely top-heavy abominable snowman.

I roll over onto my back and undo the latches on the pack once again. Sitting up, I notice that this cache box is a different style from the previous ones. Where those were sleek and aerodynamic, this one is squat and bulky. I flick open the latches and notice that they, too, are different. The previous ones gave off a satisfying, solid-sounding low G. These ones give off a high, condescending F that pierces my ears under my toque. But the strange cache opens easily enough. Inside I discover something new. It's a simple, glossy paper postcard with a picture of palm trees on the front and bright blue letters proclaiming: *Aloha from Hawaii!* I flip it over and immediately recognize the jerky, clumsy handwriting, see the date and realize it was written only a few days ago.

So, he's not dead yet.

> *Dearest Charles,*
> *We both know what you're trying to do and we both know that you won't succeed. One weekend in Ottawa can't possibly*

be enough. *What you're trying to do to me won't work. I'm going to pull through this just like before. And then, after you fail, I'm going to go up there and do it right and then all those bastards will pay up. Every last penny. But you should forget about the money. Their lawyers and accountants will never actually agree to it. They were just putting on a good show for the media.*

The world might be watching you and cheering you on, but I know you for the back-stabbing hypocrite you are.

Good luck once you hit open ice. You might discover the caches are a little harder to find up there.

Your loving brother,

Lawrence

P.S. *I'll be sure to give your love to Sandy.*

I laugh then, sitting there in the middle of the desolation, thinking about Larry back home in his hospital bed, thinking about how completely pissed off he's going to be when I show up in Russia alive and well in a few months.

I eat as much as I damn well please of the self-heating meatloaf and mashed potatoes with apple crumble for dessert, then I fill my bag with more energy bars, some salt packets, a few protein crackers and some juice crystals. I have yet to make any juice on this journey, but the crystals are great just to snack on, to melt in my mouth while lying in the cold tent after a long, cold day.

Larry's postcard is lying palm trees up on the ice and I decide to leave it there. Maybe human eyes will never see it again or maybe, through some fluke of geology and the environment, it'll get preserved in the ice somehow and some archaeologist will find it in a few millennia. At any rate, I've got enough reminders of my little brother to keep me going for years.

Re-motivated, I get up and start walking again. For all I know it could be eleven-thirty at night, but I'm not tired so it's not time to pitch the tent yet.

The cold, as always, causes my joints to ache, but I try to think of it more as a reminder of my childhood, as an old friend, rather than an annoyance.

As I walk, I wonder how Larry managed to get that postcard in there when the caches should all have been deposited a couple of weeks ago. But he's a resourceful guy, capable of pulling off magic tricks from thousands of kilometres away, even bedridden. I think about my little brother and that first contact I've had with him since starting this journey, and I wonder what the hell I'm doing in the Arctic Circle. Me! This is *me* doing this and not him. This is me only one week in, still technically on Canadian soil, or rock or something anyway, a couple of metres below the ice I'm walking on. Me: the first person to attempt a solo walk across the Arctic Circle.

I look behind me at the sun and realize it isn't getting any dimmer. I pick up my pack and keep walking and I wonder if Sandra will ever forgive me.

I keep walking and I think: people always assumed Larry was the crazy one.

T W O

$\mathcal{F}$OR A LONG TIME I WONDERED IF THIS WHOLE THING
wasn't really our dad's idea.

It was early fall. There were a few outstanding minor issues from
our mother's will, a few unresolved details that required of us not
so much correct interpretation as mutually agreed-upon misunder-
standing. It was utterly impossible to read our mother's mind when
she was alive, so you could just forget about trying to decipher her
handwritten intentions more than a year after her death. Larry had
the better lawyers, of course, but thanks to his general lack of interest in our mother's life, hospitalization and death, I had been able
to steer the proceedings and, as far as such a thing was possible,
see that things went the way I think my mother would have wanted.
Her house was finally up for sale but the little details were still
nagging at me and I wanted to take care of them. So, I went to visit
my brother at his house in North York, the seven-bedroom behemoth
with a backlot facing onto the ravine, in which he usually resided
when he was in town. I hadn't been able to get him on the phone,
but I had interpreted his secretary's aloofness and reluctance to tell

me where he was to mean that he was probably around. I figured I'd take a chance.

The exterior of the house was comically ostentatious, the kind of thing that only my brother, or someone like him, could think was a good idea. There were five distinct outdoor art pieces on his front lawn in addition to two unrelated in-ground fountains, one slate, one tiled. None of the statuary seemed to be from the same century or the same artist. One of them was a miniature wrought-iron unicorn.

My brother lived alone but his house was huge. And ugly. It was ugly before he bought it, but it got even uglier once he was finished putting mismatched blinds on the windows, installing an awkwardly situated stone wall and painting gold trim in random places—around the doorframe, across the railing, even on an occasional paving stone in the pathway up to the house.

I rang the doorbell and waited. For all his wealth, Larry never had any assistants or servants and probably preferred to be alone. Jaimie, his secretary, was strictly a part of the corporation for which he worked. In his private life there was never anyone to give my brother a hand or to look after things for him. Not now that our mother was gone, anyway.

Still, he really could have used someone to come by and do his gardening.

I rang the bell again and pressed my ear to the door to discern if it was working, and then heard what sounded like a diesel motor come to life around the side of the house. I walked to the back and found my brother seated on a John Deere forklift, hoisting a piece of limestone the size of a small couch onto an unsteady pile of similar rocks. There was a flock of birds, somehow undisturbed by the noise of the machine, sitting in a tree next to him, peering down at his work. I went over to get his attention, but he was focused on what he was doing and didn't see me until the rock was carefully balanced on top and he was backing away to get a better look at his creation. When he saw me he turned off the motor and climbed down.

"Charlie, you're in my backyard," he said.

"That's right, Larry. Hi. Good afternoon. How are you?" My brother looked just like he always did, his thick glasses askew, his short, dark hair a mess, a couple days' growth of beard on his cheeks and his teeth an uninviting shade of yellow.

"I'm making an Inukshuk," he said. I looked behind me and could now see what he was trying to do. "Remember? Like Mom used to have in the garden?"

"Or that one down by Lakeshore?"

"Yes, exactly, Charlie. Like that one. That was to celebrate a World Youth Day back in 2002. And to welcome a pope. The artist is still alive, you know. I asked him to make me one just like it, but he wouldn't do it, so I'm making my own. I want to make something that will last forever. If this one works out, maybe I'll make ten of them and send them around the country. One to each province. They can keep them forever."

I went over and stood beside my brother, did my best to make it look like I was appreciating his work. I crossed my arms and leaned forward, squinting with what I hoped looked to him like an over-exaggerated critic's appraisal. "It's really great, Larry," I lied.

In general, I really like Inukshuks and I truly think they look like people. Our mom had a miniature one in her garden when we were growing up. Sure, they tend to have inhumanly squat bodies and sometimes, for structural reasons, their arms have to come out of their abdomens, but I think that if one ever came to life I'd go sit with it under a tree and we'd smoke a pipe—or whatever rock creatures do to relax—and I'd ask it about all the secrets of life and the universe. Or about the planet Earth anyway. Surely billion-year-old rocks must know a whole lot they're not telling us.

So, in general, I think they're pretty cool and friendly looking. However, my brother had somehow constructed a bizarre and frightening rock-monster that looked like a sea serpent doing its best impression of a human being.

"I think it needs a better head," said Larry. As he spoke, the grotesque pile of rocks started to lean forward. I grabbed my brother and pulled him back just as the top-heavy creature smashed to the ground, the largest centre stone cracking precisely in two. The flock of birds took flight to seek less mobile stone statues, swearing loudly at us in an orchestra of As and B-flats.

I arranged the features of my face into a mime of disappointment so that Larry couldn't miss that I felt bad. And, in a not-insignificant way, I guess I did.

"Well," he said. "Good thing I rented the forklift for three days." He leaned over and brushed limestone dust from his hands onto his pants. "Would you like to have a beer?"

The question took me by surprise, but I didn't let that show. My brother is the world's worst host at the best of times. To be asked to stick around for a beer after a fiasco of Inukshuk proportions was weird. "Okay," I said. And I was surprised again to realize I was eager to have a beer with my brother.

He went back into the house and I walked over to the fallen body. It looked like nothing more now than some irregularly placed, vaguely rectangular stones, each the size of a large coffin. I climbed up on the piece that had broken, half of which was lying in the shade of a giant northern pine.

When we were kids, Larry would often undertake projects without thinking them through. He didn't have many friends growing up because of his social disability, but he managed to keep himself entertained. Once he used string and coat hangers to build a Rube Goldberg machine that would fry two eggs for my dad as soon as he opened his bedroom door in the morning. Another time he built one that would start Dad's car in the winter, but that ended up with the green '07 Sentra crashing through the garage door and out into traffic, so Larry had to promise not to do anything like that any more. Instead, he took to doing home renovations without permission. For a whole two weeks when I was a kid and my parents were on vacation in the Aleutians I can remember not having any railing on the second floor above the stairs. Our grandmother was looking after us but she couldn't climb stairs so she didn't notice it was gone. Larry had removed it to make it better somehow, and so there was this yawning chasm right outside the door to my bedroom, six metres straight down to the main floor. Since I used to be worried about sleepwalking, I took to tying my ankle to my bedpost before bed. He got in a bit of trouble when our folks got home but, really, if it had been *me* who removed the railing, I would have been grounded for a year. At least I could learn from mistakes like that, but talking to Larry about why some of his ideas were flawed most often got you nowhere. Growing up with him was usually a lot like that: like trying to communicate with a being made of stone.

A broken one.

"Hey!" he called from the house. "How about a glass of wine instead?"

I really didn't want a glass of wine. "Sure!" I yelled back.

He returned with an open bottle of ice-cold chardonnay and two glasses, poured me far too much, then climbed up onto the part of the split stone that had landed in the sun. "I'll probably try again tomorrow," he said, kicking his feet against the broken abdomen beneath him.

"No work?"

"On vacation." The guy not only made millions a year doing practically nothing as far as I could see, but he also seemed to be on permanent vacation.

"All week?"

He looked at me and I almost thought for a second that he was just a normal person, capable of interacting with other human beings on a regular, socially fluid scale. "For as long as I want," he said, and finished off his entire glass of wine, put it down and leaned back on his hands, surveying the destruction around us.

"How's Katelyn?" he asked. Again, this was an astonishingly strange question coming from my brother. Since when did he care about my personal life? I wondered if there wasn't something seriously wrong with his head. Or—looking at the glass—maybe he was just drunk.

"No, uh. We broke up about six months ago. Sorry, I thought I told you." In fact, I knew I had told him twice.

"Oh, no, I guess. Well, maybe you did," he said dismissively in that irritated voice he brought out whenever his limitations broke the surface.

There was something going on with Larry, but I didn't know what. The wine he had drank—my brother is actually better when he's been drinking—combined with the strange mood he was in tempted me to tread into very tender territory. "Are *you* seeing anyone, Larry?" I braced myself for a backlash, but his façade remained solid.

"Actually no, I'm not. But I started with a consulting service this week."

"A what?"

"To help me meet someone. A woman."

"Oh. Like, a dating service?"

"No," he said with only minor disdain, "to help me, you know, maybe meet someone online. They help you."

My brother was the only person I knew who had trouble meeting people through the Internet. Of course, he was the only person I'd ever known with so many personal problems. And I wondered what brought him to consider this course of action, to consider taking some positive, active steps towards meeting someone. I felt, as the older brother...and with Mom gone...that I should probably be encouraging.

"That's really great, I think, Larry. I mean, yeah. I really think that—"

"I have cancer again."

The broken stone underneath me swayed to the side but I put my hand down to hold it steady. It was warm outside for autumn in Toronto, a cloudless, bright day. The birds had not returned since the stone catastrophe, and the complete silence in the middle of the day was no doubt what caused the property values in the neighbourhood to go so high.

It didn't seem like the right kind of day for my brother to have cancer.

"Jesus, Larry," I said. "Wow." Wow. "Wow. I'm...I'm really sorry, man. That's awful. Where...?"

He didn't look over at me, just gently tapped the side of his head. Head cancer?

"Brain?" I asked.

He nodded slowly.

"Oh. Wow, Larry, wow. Wow. That really sucks. Really. Is it—?"

"I have one year only to live," he said.

I finished off the wine in my glass, reached for the bottle and poured myself another. Brain cancer. That explained the indefinite vacation.

"I can probably extend it," he said. "Maybe I can get a year and a half. Maybe two." And if those assertions had been made by anyone else but Larry, I would have discounted them as statements of denial. But with Larry I figured he was probably right. He probably really could outlive the predictions.

Larry had beaten cancer twice already.

"Brain cancer, Charlie. Different. A bad one. The doctors say this is it. They don't think I'm going to walk away from it. Not one step."

Larry and I rarely saw eye to eye. In fact, for most of our lives we were barely on talking terms. Still, when your younger brother tells you he's got a year to live, you can't help but want to reach out and put an arm on his shoulder.

But since I knew my brother I stayed on my own half of the rock.

"I want to do something before..." he said.

"Before?"

"Before I die, idiot," he said, his eyes humourless.

"No, I know. Sorry, Lar, I just mean...like what?"

"Oh. You know. Something no one's ever done. *Something*."

"Like...what?"

He sighed. I could tell he was getting impatient with me. "I don't know. But there's got to be something left, doesn't there?"

"You mean like, discover something? Invent something?" *Cure cancer?* I thought, but I didn't say it out loud.

"No, I mean, like...just go someplace, maybe. Be the first to do something, see something, or like, accomplish something. *Star Trek*. To boldly go where no man has gone before. I don't know, Charlie. Maybe you know of something." Larry's reaction to his imminent death was exactly like him. Building an Inukshuk in his backyard was exactly like him. Hell, maybe even hiring a consulting service to help him meet a woman was exactly like him. Maybe he wasn't in a strange mood after all. Maybe he was just dying. Larry might be dying and he might be dying friendless and alone, but he'd be damned if he wasn't going to do something first and a hell of a lot better than anyone has ever done it before.

"But, Larry, like what? What do you mean? Like, go to Mars?"

He laughed that dismissive, condescending laugh of his, the one I'd grown up with and grown to hate over the past thirty years, and it hit me that that was probably the last thing I'd ever hear from Larry before he died. That snide, prickish laugh. "The Mars program is still about a decade away, idiot. Not a chance. But I did think about being the first civilian to land on the moon maybe, but no. The preparation time for that would still be too much."

We sat in silence then. It was easy to sit quietly with Larry when he was thinking. It was very difficult to be around the guy when he was trying to be social, but when he was deep in thought he could be as remote as the Himalayas.

My butt was getting sore underneath me, but it wasn't anything that another half glass of wine wouldn't help. So we sat in silence and I thought about our mom, about how she lived to see her youngest son survive cancer twice only to be taken by it herself. Maybe it wasn't the worst thing in the world that she left when she did, rather than painfully hanging on for another year, just to see Larry suffer again. I may not get along with my whole family, but I had really loved my mother.

I really missed my mom.

"What about swimming along the floor of the deepest part of the ocean?" he said, eventually.

"You mean the very bottom?"

"Yeah, wherever that is. The very, very bottom. Swim around outside of a vessel?"

"I don't think that's possible yet, Larry."

"But with a year to prepare? To build the proper equipment?"

"Maybe. I don't know. Maybe you can do it. You're a smart guy. But it seems really hard to me." Silence again then, and I knew he was trying to work out the logistics, trying with that enormous, brilliant, flawed brain of his to figure out if a year was enough time to build a suit capable of sustaining human life on the very bottom of the deepest ocean. My brother, sitting on a broken piece of stone beside me, had brain cancer, and he was using his remaining time on the planet to figure out if he could make it to the bottom of the sea before he died. It seemed weird to me, but could I say I would live my final days any differently?

"No, I don't think I can do it," he concluded eventually. "Not in a year anyway."

"So what then, Larry?"

"I dunno. I was thinking maybe...who was that guy that Dad always admired?"

"Um, Alex Trebek?" Our dad, a loud but wonderful Russian immigrant who had died from a heart attack just before I graduated high school, had always been a passionate *Jeopardy!* fan. It was one of the things I remembered most vividly about him.

"No, idiot. Not Trebek. The Arctic guy."

"Oh, that guy. Weber. You mean Richard Weber?"

"Yeah."

"What about him?"

"Well, I don't know. What if I did something like him?"

"Well, you'd really have to look into it, but I think he's done it all."

"Gone to the North Pole on skis? What about with no resupplies? What about on foot?"

"Yeah, I think so, man. I think he did all of that stuff."

I tried to remember what my dad had said about Weber, about how the guy had done everything there was left to do in the North Pole. My dad grew up in Murmansk and immigrated to Whitehorse when he was a teenager and he'd always loved the north. When we were younger our family had gone on vacation to *all* of the northern countries. But Dad had wanted to see the North Pole with his own eyes. And, for that matter, "I remember once he said he wanted to walk between the countries. From the Arctic Circle on Canadian soil to the Arctic Circle in Russia. You know, across the Pole." At least, I thought I remembered him saying something like that once.

"Really?"

"I think so."

"Huh. Yeah. Huh. Charles. Has anyone ever done that before?"

"I don't know. I think I remember Dad talking about it, maybe. About wanting to do it. Just getting up one day when he was a kid in the Yukon, waking up in the morning and walking from Canada to Russia. But I don't know. I doubt anyone's ever done that before. It doesn't seem likely. It's probably really, really far."

"Yeah, maybe."

"Plus, you know, you probably weren't able to do it for a long time."

"What do you mean?"

"Well, it probably takes a while. And before, you know, when the Arctic ice would melt in the summer, when the Gulf Stream was still active. Climate change and all that." Larry didn't respond but I could see he was thinking. I could easily have left then without saying goodbye and it might have taken him an hour or so to notice my absence—if he noticed at all. I still hadn't digested the fact that my brother was dying, but I knew that it was a good time to leave. Whenever I got a chance to leave my brother on good terms I liked to take it. Besides, with his news, it seemed wrong to bring up those few outstanding minor details from our mother's will. Our mother, who had died only fourteen months ago from cancer.

I got up. "Thanks for the wine." I placed my empty glass on a flat part of the stone.

He snapped out of his reverie. "Okay. Hey, Charlie? Why don't you come by next week?" He kicked the stone under him and smiled. "You can see the finished product."

"All right," I said. Treading thin ice again, I held out my palm to him. My brother looked at it and—maybe it was the wine—he didn't pause before grasping it in his own and shaking my hand.

"Thanks, Charlie," he said. "You're really a great brother."

If it wasn't for the absolute silence all around us I would have stood there speechless for an hour, just shaking his hand without stopping, as though I too had some sort of social disability, and wondering if I had heard him correctly.

THREE

IT'S A WEEK BEFORE I FIND ANOTHER MESSAGE IN A FOOD cache from Lawrence. *Beautiful Argentina* it says across the bottom. Four glossy images on its front show: a lighthouse on a tropical island, a field of cactuses, a waterfall and a whale jumping out of the water.

> *Dearest Charlie,*
>
> *The media reports on you remain hopeful. The consensus is that the corporations will pay your demands, but only if you succeed. When you fail, they will most definitely renege. Don't worry, I can make sure that happens.*
>
> *I'm getting better. The doctors have extended my deadline again, but I knew they would. Doctors are always so pessimistic.*
>
> *After you fail I'm going to do it right, with a video camera so that everyone knows.*
>
> *Your recuperating brother,*
>
> *Lawrence*
>
> P.S. *Your house burned to the ground last week. Nothing was saved.*

By the time I find this cache I'm exhausted and starving. There's only one cache per day and since I missed the one yesterday I've been living off energy bars, juice crystals and stored energy for almost a hundred kilometres. Today I only managed to go forty-five klicks. Not enough. Five klicks I'm going to have to make up somewhere between here and the Pole. I figure it's only going to get harder on the other side.

I sit down with my back to the cold, eternal sun. The cold is a constant presence, un-ignorable. It's not like when you go to an animal pavilion at the zoo and at first it smells really bad but then you get used to it. No. You never get used to this cold, and that's probably a good thing.

I check the cache and find spaghetti and meatballs, something that calls itself garlic bread that Larry loves and knows I can't stand. A self-heating Italian meal at the top of the world. I guess it could be worse. He could have tried to keep with the northern theme and sent me Finnish food. Or Icelandic.

I activate the heating unit on the pasta, leaving the bread in the cache. Maybe some needy Inuit will find it sometime and wonder what the hell garlic is. Man, would it be nice to meet some friendly Inuit dude. I find that it's the human company I miss the most. Maybe my brother was right. Maybe I should have brought a video camera or at least some sort of device that would allow me to communicate with the outside world. Then at least I could find out if my house really did burn down or if he wrote that to piss me off. I can't deny that the thought is distracting.

There's oatmeal for the morning. Just add ice and the packaging takes care of the rest. Some sort of chemical reaction inside the container. I really don't care how it works. All I want is hot food. I also find the usual coffee, which I've generally been ignoring but I'm feeling tired today and don't want to rest quite yet. From the side of my sack I take the pick-axe, a wonderful little tool that weighs practically nothing and is strong enough to chop through office doors or Arctic rock—I've seen it done. I cut a fist-sized piece of ice from the floor beneath me, tear open the top of the coffee container, drop it in and seal it. Recollections from my Arctic survival training course remind me that the coffee's going to taste salty, but I haven't seen any clear blue ice for a few days. There's a hissing noise and steam escapes from a little spout on one side. I hadn't noticed the slight breeze to my back, but it carries the steam almost twenty centimetres before the vapour crystallizes and falls down onto my boots. The coffee will keep itself warm for five or ten minutes, so I undo my pack and lodge it under my side. I'm due for a short rest anyway.

Overall I'm making really great time. Averaging just under fifty klicks a day, the whole trek should be close to or just over a hundred days. There's no way explorers last century could have made fifty klicks a day on foot, but then they had to stop and prepare their own meals once in a while, and they didn't have energy bars or GPS systems to keep them on a straight path. I'm going just over five thousand klicks without skis or dogsled or Ski-Doo so I need all the help I can get. People can do the Iditarod in under ten days, and that's close to two thousand kilometres over similar terrain. If I had dogs with me, I could do this whole thing in less than a month.

But of course, that was never in the plan. Larry's never liked dogs.

Instead it's only me, three months alone in the Arctic. And the GPS says I'm still on actual, physical land, though I've been walking on frozen river beds for the most part because the terrain is flat and easy. I haven't crossed onto what used to be called the Ward Hunt ice shelf yet. That's not going to happen for over another week at least. The GPS shows that within a few days I should be in sight of an abandoned radar detection installation, old Cold War stuff that hasn't worked in decades but is still there because it would cost the government too much money to disassemble. And that was *before* the economy took a dive.

The spaghetti's the best I've ever had—north of seventy degrees north latitude—and I think that maybe I'll save an extra bit of food from one of the caches and hole up at the radar site for a day. Maybe there'll be a bunker or something with a genuine, metal-framed cot I could sleep on. Night after night on the cold ice with only the tent floor, a thin mattress and my sleeping bag had already been getting old after the first night.

I drink the coffee slowly and try to make the pasta last. It partially freezes as I lift the fork to my mouth and I wonder, not for the first time, about how crazy it is to be attempting an Arctic crossing in the summer. Earlier in my own lifetime, the Arctic would have been completely thawed by this time of the year. Water at the North Pole. Scientists first predicted this would happen in the summer of 2008, but it didn't actually come about until over a decade later. Prior to that there hadn't been an ice-free north for over 700,000 years. Seven. Hundred. *Thousand.* Years. But then humans came along, invented society and industry and "progress," and in a relatively short time managed to thaw the whole damn thing. Global warming, they said. Now, of course, the reverse has happened. Now the entire Arctic Ocean is frozen all year long. Climate change is a tricky little bitch. Thawing the ice cap stopped the North Atlantic from drawing the warm waters of the Gulf Stream up, and now the Arctic Ocean and much of Europe is experiencing something like a Little Ice Age, though much more severe than the one that ended in the eighteenth century. This one seems like it's going to last a heck of a lot longer...

It's colder than ever up here but I've got, or at least I hope I've got, the right equipment to keep me alive. The planes from Canada and Russia dropped off the food caches weeks ago. They're waiting out there for me to pick them up. And as long as I keep moving I should be all right. No open water up ahead, not until Russia anyway. No eternal darkness to worry about.

I reflect for the first time that, in addition to diametrically crossing the Arctic Circle on foot, I'm doing something else that even Richard Weber had never done: travelling to the North Pole in the middle of the summer.

When I finish dinner I get up and start walking again. I check the GPS to make sure I'm heading in the right direction, to see how much farther it is until the next cache. Fifty kilometres by this time tomorrow. One one-hundredth of the entire trip.

I hoist my pack and think—not for the first time—that I should have been carrying the equipment by sled rather than pack. But at least my shoulders no longer complain. They're silent on the matter. Maybe they've learned that everything inside is a valuable necessity. More likely they've simply lost the will to voice their opinion.

It sounds silly to me now but somehow, when I was starting out, the whole journey didn't seem that long at just over five thousand kilometres. "Only" roughly half the extreme width of Canada. Three time zones' worth, say. And, really, lots of people either walk or jog or run or cycle across our enormous country every year, don't they? How hard should it be to do half of that? Fifty kilometres or so per day, a hundred days straight across the Arctic Circle from Canada to Russia—a piece of cake.

I don't even have brain cancer to slow me down.

Of course, my mind drifts back home then, back to my house, to my things, wondering if they're all okay or if they're all truly burned to cinders in my absence. My piano, my antique books, my neat crystal scotch bottle with the C.I.A. crest, my clarinet I've had since I was a kid.

The map books my father gave me.

Maybe they're all gone now. Maybe I'll never see them again.

Then again, I think, exhaling the sharp, sub-zero oxygen from my lungs and trying to calculate how far I have yet to go...then again, maybe everything's still all right back home. Maybe everything's fine and Sandra's forgiven me and my piano is not burned to a crisp. Maybe.

I look ahead of me at the nothing of the Arctic and think: Even if everything is just fine back there, maybe I'll still never see them again.

FOUR

*I*T WAS OCTOBER, JUST BEFORE THE THANKSGIVING weekend. Despite telling my brother I'd see him soon I hadn't gone back to visit for almost three weeks. Things had kept coming up. I had work to do, more clients than usual. By the time I finally cleared enough space to visit Larry it was the day before I was supposed to go endurance hiking with a couple of old friends from university and I had a lot to pack and to do and was on my way out of town with a cold case of Keith's in the trunk. But the Don Valley Parkway was completely blocked and I was forced to cut across town to get to Highway 400, and then I found myself in Larry's neighbourhood and, well, I really wanted to see how that Inukshuk had turned out.

I parked the car and went up to his door. I still didn't know if his doorbell worked, so after three fruitless tries I showed myself around back. The forklift was gone but otherwise everything was exactly how it was when I had left. Even my wine glass was still sitting on the split stone, half-full of mucky water and leaves. The flock of birds had returned to the tree and had done a good job over the weeks of painting the stones white. I wondered if Larry had left town and figured I should have called first.

"Charlie!"

I looked up. Larry was calling to me from one of the windows on his second floor. I waved and his head disappeared. He reappeared at the back door and invited me in. "There's someone you could meet," he said. The first thing I noticed about him was that his hair was strange. My brother had never learned to style his hair. It's not that he would have been incapable of it, but it was exactly the kind of thing he would need someone to remind him to do. Standing in his back foyer, however, it looked as though he had done his best to style it, giving it as much thought as he gave to making an Inukshuk. He must have taken a handful of hair gel and plastered it all to his scalp. I considered offering to fix it for him, but didn't want to give offence.

He walked swiftly to the stairs and I assumed, from years of experience, that I was to follow him.

The second floor of Larry's house was one big office. Well, technically five medium-size offices, what a real estate agent would probably have called "bedrooms," but each held at least two computers. One had a drafting table and tools, one had a floor-to-ceiling blackboard, one had models of chromosomes or proteins or something, one had what looked like a disassembled toaster, and one had Sandra.

I stopped.

"This is her," said Larry.

And she looked at me.

My first thought was that she was stunning. Quite literally. She stunned me. Like I was hit with some kind of freeze ray. As though all the cells in my body took a momentary pause before the Earth, spinning somehow on its axis, could thrust me back into the world of time and movement. She *stunned* me.

My second thought was: how can she possibly walk around like that all day, stunning people wherever she went? Wouldn't it get annoying? She gets into a cab and the driver can't pull away from the curb for a few seconds because he's frozen in time. I guess it might come in handy with muggers, though. They stop you on the street to take your purse, you flash your smile at them and then take off in the other direction before they have a chance to recover. Some kind of capacity to freeze the souls of men right inside their bodies.

My third thought was that I should probably say something to her.

"Oh, um, hi," I said. "Charles."

This was the woman that Larry had managed to meet? This woman used the *Internet*? I made a mental note that I *really* had to stop going out so much. The strategy from then on was going to be: stay at home and spend as much time on the computer as possible.

"Hi," she said. "I'm Sandra, Larry's consultant." We shook hands. Her palm was as warm as the centre of the sun. Or buttered toast or a horse or something.

She was just so *damn* good-looking.

"Oh," I said. "Right, of course. You're helping him..."

"Improve his online persona."

"Well, a nice guy like my brother, it couldn't be too difficult," I said, with the tiniest note of sarcasm. I wasn't sure she would pick up on it, but I could see in her eyes that she did. Larry didn't have a chance.

"You're too nice, my brother," he said.

Her hair was a million different colours which, when put together, came off as a sort of bright, brownish-blondish mass that all you wanted to do was run your hands through or cover yourself in or, if nothing else, at least get a chance to smell.

And I realized that what I was feeling was probably what my brother must feel around real people all the time: a simple inability to look them in the eye, a tendency to stutter over words, a desire simply to go back to my bedroom in the basement and read computer manuals and play Dungeons and Dragons.

"Anyway, I was just leaving. There's no need to walk me out," she said—though she said it to me and not to Larry. So she already knew that Larry wasn't the type of person to walk someone to his door? How long had she been coming around here? "I'll see you next week, Larry. I'll bring my camera, we'll take photos, okay?"

"Okay," he said.

"Do you want me to write it down?"

"No!" he said, a bit too loudly.

"All right then. It was nice to meet you, Charles." And then she left, and the world sealed up around the vacuum she left behind, the sound of her bare feet padding down the carpeted stairs drifting up like the softest, most finely tuned percussion instrument in the world.

I sat down.

"That's my consultant," said my brother. "Sandra. You met her."

"Thanks," I said. "Yeah." Larry sat down too, smiling, and I could see he was proud of himself for taking this step, for reaching out to real people, for now, finally, trying to get some help, trying to meet someone. "So how's it going?" I asked, meaning the Internet woman search.

"Fine," he said. "No pain. Still one year to live."

Oh, right. The brain cancer. I put on an exaggerated big-brother-caring-for-you face. "Still think you're going to beat that?"

"Oh, for sure," he said. "I'm going to walk across the Arctic Circle."

It was all I could do not to laugh. Not that he would have taken it the wrong way. On the contrary, it would have been one of those rare times when he would rightly have flown off the handle for someone laughing at him. "When are you leaving?" I asked.

"Next summer. You were right. With climate change I can do it in the summer, it'll be frozen until the Russian coast."

"How far is it?"

"Five-thousand, two-hundred and sixty kilometres. The route will go over frozen rivers on the land, then around the coast of Ellesmere. That way there won't be anything in the way. It'll be almost a straight line."

"On foot? You think you can do that?"

"No one's ever done it before." He was serious. I knew it right then: my brother was serious about walking across the diameter of the Arctic Circle. Walking. *On foot.* You'd have to be crazy to try something like that.

"I can do it," he said, still smiling, still proud of himself in a way; it was a confidence that I hadn't seen in him since we were little kids, skipping stones across the lake by our uncle's cottage or him beating me in video games.

"Huh," I said. It's weird how you grow up together with someone and, all along, maybe you do realize that you yourself are growing. One day you're a kid and then one day you're an adult. It's weirder the day you realize that your younger brother, the kid you had to protect your whole life, is, in his own way, some kind of an adult too.

"Dad would be proud of you," I said, and realized it was true. And, as I said it, I wanted to embrace my prickish, dying little brother.

"I know," he said, smiling. And that, more than anything, brought tears to my eyes.

"You'll be all right Larry. You know that? I only came by to see how you were doing."

"I'm doing all right!" he asserted, as though there were any other possibility in the world. He hated it when people worried about him.

"All right, Lar, I know. I know. Anyway, I was in the neighbourhood. I'm going hiking for the weekend, but how about if I drop by next week, maybe Thursday night?"

"Okay, sure. Write it down?" I wrote it down for him on a notepad on the nearest desk, though how he'd find it among everything else in this, just one of five offices, I wasn't sure. Then I showed myself out, no need for goodbyes with my brother. Sometimes they only confuse him.

It had gotten darker since I went inside but, waiting by my car, she was still impossible to miss.

"Your brother," she said.

"Yes?"

"Is he all right?"

"I...I don't even know how to begin answering that question."

She obviously didn't know how to take that. "I mean, like... Does he have...maybe some kind of disorder?"

Treacherous territory. Thin ice. Who was this woman? "He hasn't told you?"

"No, he hasn't mentioned anything."

"Then why do you ask?"

"Well, he seems, well, different."

"How so?"

"Differently social, I mean."

"Huh."

"So there is something?"

"I'm sorry, I really don't think I should be speaking on behalf of my brother. Why don't you ask him?"

"I tried once, subtly. It took him a long time to realize what I was driving at, then he got...rather upset." That's my brother. "So, really, anything you can tell me would be helpful."

"I'm sorry, I just don't think I should get involved."

"Is it Asperger Syndrome?" Well. That was that, then. I said nothing.

"I thought so," she concluded.

"Well." We stood there by my car for a few seconds and I wondered if I should give her my card or something. Just in case she ever needed to contact me. Just in case.

"Your brother says you're in the music industry," she said and I laughed.

"That's nice of him."

"Do you play anything?"

"Yeah, I play a bit. Sometimes with the symphony."

"The TSO?"

"Yeah."

"What do you play?"

"Woodwinds, usually the flute. Whenever someone's sick. Mainly, though, I'm a music therapist."

Shockingly, she didn't provide me with the common response, which was to ask if that was a real job. "So you help people who have suffered from traumas that inhibit their musical ability? Get them back on track?"

"That's...actually, that's pretty much exactly what I do."

"Maybe you'd like to get together for a coffee sometime?"

Of course I did. What, was I a rotting corpse in the ground, some sort of stone-faced monster incapable of human feeling? But why? "To talk about Larry?"

"It would be helpful, I think," she said.

"Sorry," I said. "I really think I should stay away from that. Good luck with my brother," I said and only when the words were out of my mouth did I realize what a hard job this woman must have. Trying to find a date for *Larry*. Even on the Internet that was a rather Herculean task. Or Amazonian, as the case may be. Whichever.

"Oh, come on," she said. "I don't *really* want to talk about your brother."

Oh. "Oh," I said. And then it just came out of me: "Did he tell you he was *dying*?"

She shook her head. I could also see that the answer was no.

"All right. *All right*. You've spent some time with him. Here it is: he's got brain cancer and he wants to walk across the Arctic Circle. Fine. All right. Maybe we *should* talk. But, you know, he kind of drives me nuts a lot of the time. So I'd rather not talk only about Larry."

"So...what are we going to talk about?"

"I don't know," I said. "Maybe we can figure it out later."

We exchanged numbers and made a dinner date for the next Thursday. And that was how I met Sandra.

FIVE

"Hello?"

I'm still asleep, or trying to be.

"Someone alive in there?"

I open my eyes and notice that it's dark outside. Sweet, glorious dark. How I've longed for the darkness of night for about a month now but eternal Sun in his constant, imperial orbit won't grant it to me. Oh, Lord Sun, why will you not let me rest!

"Hello?"

I moan something in return. Someone's calling something to me. Someone alive outside of my tent? Is it possible? I hear the struts shake and my warmth is disturbed. I reach my hand out of my sleeping bag and pull it away, squint my eyes at the light streaming in. It's not dark outside after all; it's the same as always. A long, vague shadow is cast on what I assume to be the south wall of the tent.

"Who is it?" I ask.

"People," states what sounds like a woman. She sounds young.

"Minute," I say, and begin the involved task of removing myself from the sleeping bag. It's double-zipped, made of the same impervious material as my gloves. I've been finding it warm enough in the sleeping bag to sleep in nothing but shorts. This makes it difficult to put on clothes quickly though, because it's still less than zero degrees in the still air of the tent and I don't like getting dressed where my body parts can freeze and fall off. But for now I make a few sacrifices of comfort for speed, pull on my innerwear, then my outerwear. The GPS said it was only supposed to be minus twenty today, so I opt to skip the headgear in the name of expediency. I touch my hair and then, for the first time in almost a month, I wonder what I look like.

Some strange, possibly young, possibly attractive woman is standing outside my tent. Possibly this and possibly that, yes, but *definitely* a woman. Well, and definitely strange. I'm in a tent in the Arctic Circle, after all.

My hair feels like a mess but I had seen no reason to bring a mirror with me and nothing in my equipment strikes me as sufficient for the purpose. I realize I have a month's growth of beard—and my beard is horribly patchy—but there's nothing I can do about that, either.

Maybe Larry has the advantage in this one. He never worries about what he looks like. I sigh, pull on my toque, and crawl out of the tent.

At first I think: well, I sure was mistaken. A man is standing three metres away, looking sceptically at me. His beard is about as patchy as mine and, though it's hard to tell behind his goggles, he's got to be only in his mid-twenties.

And then I see the woman—woman as bundle of androgynous snow gear—standing behind my tent—the figure who was casting a shadow upon it. Again, hard to tell how old she is, or if she's attractive or not—snow queen or ice goblin—and I reflect that not only have I not shaved in a month but neither have I gotten laid.

"How's it going?" she asks.

And all I can think to say is: "Good."

She smiles at this and walks over, holds out her hand. "Cecilia Pine."

"I'm Charles Perth," I say, expecting a reaction. Everyone back home has heard of me. Everyone in Canada, Russia, pretty much the entire civilized world. The guy who's walking alone across the Arctic Circle. From the two of them I get no reaction.

"What's happened to your glove?" she asks.

I look down at the bright pink thumb, think about how often over the past three weeks I've been holding it out to imaginary transport trucks hoping for a lift, wondering if it would void the corporate contracts if I accepted a ride. "I had an accident."

"With a diamond-edged razorblade? Tritons are impossible to cut."

"I have a really good knife," I say.

"Huh."

"Paul McCartney," says the man, now standing beside me.

"Paul McCartney? Like the musician?" I ask, shaking his hand.

"No," he says sternly, and I agree that he's right.

"What are you doing way up here?" asks Cecilia Pine.

"I'm, um...you know? Walking across the Arctic Circle?"

"You're walking across the what?"

"You're what across the Arctic Circle?"

"Yeah. You know. The North Pole? Then on to Russia."

"Russia," says the man who isn't a former Beatle.

"In about two months from now maybe, yeah, if I'm lucky." If I don't freeze to death. If the GPS holds together. If I don't miss two consecutive food caches. If the ice doesn't crack or melt. If I don't die from boredom and misery and loneliness.

And can one die from celibacy?

I notice for the first time the long-range rifle in Cecilia's hand. "Um?" I ask, but I'm not sure she hears me.

"Polar bears," says Paul.

I almost—*almost*—laugh at him. "This far north?"

"Climate change is a crazy bitch," he says. "There hasn't been open water around here for years, but sometimes the bears don't know that. You should be careful out here. You have a gun?"

"No." No, I don't have a gun. It hadn't even occurred to me. As far as I knew I wasn't going into the territory of any Arctic predators—polar bears, wolves, lynxes. Not that lynxes would usually go after humans, but still. All these animals moved their habitats hundreds of klicks south after the freeze. And how well would I be welcomed across the Russian border if I was carrying a gun?

"You should be careful out here," he repeats and walks away about ten metres, stops, then urinates in the snow.

"Well," says Cecilia, "if you're just passing through, you may as well come down and spend the night with us. The food's not great, but it's *gotta* be better than whatever you're carrying around with you."

I refrain from telling them about the food caches. If they really don't know about my walk across the Arctic, there's no need to fill them in.

"Are you sure I'm allowed on the base?" I ask. "I mean, your commanding officer or whatever is cool with people dropping by unannounced?" I don't want to get involved with the armed forces if I can help it. I had thought about maybe spending a night in the bunker over at the old radar base, but not if army guys are already using it.

"We're not military," says Cecilia. I nod at the patch on her sleeve that says, clearly, Royal Military College. She shrugs. "We're just based out of there. Kingston. We're private, unaffiliated contractors to the government. We're doing an environmental impact assessment before they send up a military team to take the place apart."

"I thought the government couldn't afford to take these things down."

"Yeah, but the economy," says Paul McCartney, coming back up beside us.

"Right," I say, having almost completely forgotten, over the past month, about anything to do with the economy. Also about anything resembling commerce, business, malls, fast food, shag carpets, comfort, happiness or warmth. "The economy."

"So, come on," says Cecilia, and hoists the rifle over her shoulder. "Take your fancy tent down and come have a drink."

"Drink?"

She grins at me, the long shadows of her short eyelashes stretching across the side of her face.

"She likes her scotch," says Paul.

"Hell, I'm drunk right now," she affirms and cackles a crazy, frozen laugh that ranges from middle C to F-sharp. She pulls a stainless steel flask from her hip pocket and passes it to me.

Property of the Royal Canadian Armed Forces, it says. I look back at her and she cackles again. "It's borrowed," she says. "You can borrow it too. Come down when you're ready." And with that she walks north toward the indistinctness on the horizon. Paul McCartney lingers a moment longer as though trying to decide if he should offer to help. Then he nods, repeats, "Be careful," and follows behind Cecilia.

I look down at the flask and figure what the hell. These are the first people I've seen in almost four weeks and I'm within sight of the first real shelter I've seen in almost as long. I take a swig and feel the scotch warm my insides. Now I know why they send Saint Bernards out to find avalanche victims with little jugs of liquor tied around their necks. I take another swig but the flask is empty. I look at the two quickly shrinking silhouettes and decide that, if there's more where that came from, it's worth an imposition or two. I start to take my tent down determinedly, the scotch motivating me with a cozy glow that I haven't felt in far too long.

They seem like nice folks, those two. Paul and Cecilia. Even though she's maybe a crazy drunk, it's nice to see some people, some faces. I look down at the snow and see something else I haven't seen in almost a month: footprints that aren't my own. Paul's are about the same size as mine. Cecilia's are entirely different, though. They have a little pattern to their treads that, in the long shadows, almost look like smiley faces. They're cute little footprints that would fit quite comfortably inside mine. My footprints now seem ungainly and as boring as the sun. I now know my own footprints quite a bit *better* than I know the back of my hand. Hell, I haven't had a good look at the back of my hand in...

And then I see something else in the snow that's not my footprint. It's not Paul's footprint and it's not Cecilia's footprint.

It is, quite clearly, a relatively fresh polar bear footprint. I look closer and see that it's one of several.

And then I *really* start to take my tent down.

SIX

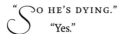

"So he's dying."

"Yes."

"From what, again?"

"Cancer. This time, of the brain."

"What do you mean, 'this time'?"

I sighed and leaned over the railing and a part of me realized I was being a bit melodramatic. Dinner had been fabulous but the conversation had been typically first-date themed. (Although perhaps it was presumptuous of me to assume that it was a first date and not a last date.) After dinner I had suggested a walk down at Ashbridge's Bay. A bit late in the year for the beach, maybe, but Sandra grew up in Burlington and had mentioned over dinner that she wished she had seen more of the city since moving here.

"This is the third time he's had cancer."

"Oh," she said. "I had no idea."

"The first time was throat cancer; the second, skin. He walked away from both of them. This one looks like it's going to be fatal, though. Even he doesn't think he can survive it, though he thinks he can outlive the doctor's estimates. Maybe he can. Still, in some ways I'm glad. At least this one's brain cancer."

Her face was orange in the light, but I could tell the colour had drained from it. "How can you say that?"

"Oh, no," I said and gently rested my hand on her forearm. "I don't mean it like that, I just mean... Look. My family is high-risk for cancer. We've known that all our lives. All four of our grandparents died from cancer. Our mom died a year and a half ago from cancer. Our dad didn't, but that's because he had a heart attack before something got him, I think. My brother, he—" I looked into her eyes and saw I wasn't making much sense. "Look, let's go sit down." We had avoided talking about Larry all night, and I figured it was about time I filled her in. We found a park bench that faced out onto the lake.

"Look," I said. "You know my brother has social problems."

"He has Asperger Syndrome," she said. "That's hardly his fault."

"All right, fine, yes. He has a disability. I *know* that. You don't have to tell me that. I grew up with the guy. All right, so he's got some social disability that he can't control. Still, he tries to overcompensate a lot of the time—"

"Oh, so that's what he's doing with me? Overcompensating?"

"*No*. No, listen. Really. I think it's great that he called you. You're probably the first active step he's taken in *ten years* to get his life in some sort of order. Really. Guy is unbelievably rich, but he can't get laid for the life of him because he doesn't know how to relate to people. Is that his fault? No, no it isn't. So the fact that he calls you up to consult and help him, hell, I think that's just great. Really, Sandra. No, that's fine. That's great. But see, he used to *really* overcompensate. He'd do anything if he thought it would make him more normal, make it seem like he fit in. Most of the time it doesn't even occur to him that he should act a certain way, so it's harmless. He doesn't think about it so it doesn't run his life and he lives obliviously but relatively happy. That's fine. But sometimes he *does* have an idea of what to do, he just goes about it all wrong."

"You mean like his hair last week?" she asked, and I see the trace of a smirk around the corners of her mouth.

"Yes," I said. "Exactly. Some tiny, socially aware part of him surfaces for a second and lets him know that 'regular' people try to make themselves presentable, maybe do their hair or something, and so his reaction is to put half a litre of hair gel on his head. Right? That's him overcompensating."

"And you're saying that one time this gave him cancer."

I looked deeply into the pores of her face to see if she was joking with me or being sincere. I didn't know her well enough to tell one way or the other, so I gave her the benefit of the doubt and nodded.

"Oh," she said. "I'm sorry."

I leaned back on the bench and prepared to tell my brother's Internet image consultant things about him that—if he were aware of it— he probably wouldn't appreciate her knowing. Of course, his social ineptitude is such that even if someone *told* him what I was telling her, there'd be a pretty decent chance he wouldn't understand it meant that Sandra's mental image of him would change as a result.

"From about grade four on he went to all-boys schools. My parents thought it would be easier for him, you know? I'm not so sure, in hindsight. It seems like he might be better today if he had more exposure to women growing up but, then, what do I know? Maybe his youth would have been so intolerable that he would have...well, anyway.

"No one knows all the details, but at some point in high school he was dragged to an inter-school dance. The teachers obviously knew about his disability—and trust me, he was a *lot* worse then—but somehow someone thought this was a good idea. Anyway, he meets a girl there. A real, live girl. I don't know how serious it was or anything, but I guess was interested in her in his own way. He does *like* women, obviously, or he wouldn't have called you."

"Obviously."

"But he doesn't know the first thing about them. Anyway, at some point or other I think she suggested that he try using mouthwash. He wanted to know why, of course. I guess she explains about personal hygiene or, hell, flat-out tells him he has bad breath, right? Anyway, for the next four years mouthwash became an obsession for him. It was all he had to go on or something. The only real, genuine clue he'd been given to how to fit in with everyone else. He would go through a bottle of mouthwash a day and I'm not exaggerating. It was the old-style low-quality stuff, too, from the dollar store. Had alcohol in it, the kind of thing you can't even buy from a drugstore anymore. He'd go on weekends and buy seven bottles. He'd use it before every class, after every meal. He wouldn't allow himself to go to sleep at night unless the bottle was finished."

"Obsessive compulsive?"

"I don't know for sure, but I don't think so. He's never been like that. I think, you know? I think he really liked this girl, some girl he met one time and who was nice enough to give him a kind word."

"And...so he got throat cancer."

I nodded again in the dim autumn evening beside the lake. "Yeah. He got throat cancer. But they caught it in time. And I wonder if even cancer would have stopped him from doing it, or if it was just that our dad told him to stop—he'd always listen to Dad."

It was only then that I realized Sandra had taken hold of my hand. At some point during my talking about Larry she had just reached over and taken it. It was perfect, sitting on the boardwalk with her, holding hands in the gathering twilight. A moment that perfect is only asking to be ruined. Better to walk away from it while it's still a real thing. "Come on," I said, and helped her to her feet.

She put her arm around mine and walked close to me. Her hair smelled so good I could have died quite happily right then. We were walking away from her car but that was right. I wished I knew what she was thinking about. Probably about life or death or something.

"The skin cancer was pretty much the same thing," I said, later. "He went to the beach one time and some girl told him he might want to use a tanning bed so he wouldn't be so pasty right at the beginning of the season."

"He is really pale," she said.

"I guess," I said. "But not for two years of his life. This was while he was away at university. We didn't see much of him, but I've seen some pictures. He was a deep orange for about sixteen months, going to tanning salons once or twice a day, sometimes skipping class to squeeze them in."

"He just wanted to fit in."

"He got cancer again."

"It's so...sad."

"Yeah, it is. Sometimes I'm glad he didn't have that many friends growing up."

"Why's that?"

"Because I know that someone, at some point, would have told him that smoking was cool or something. I really don't think he would have been able to walk away from that."

"Coming through!"

We stopped and turned and an old man with blinking elbow pads sped past us on a pair of rollerblades. He must have been all of sixty-five or seventy. Within a few seconds he was out of sight, off to parts unknown.

"Do you rollerblade?" she asked.

"Not even once in my life," I said. "Wanna get some coffee?"

"Actually..." she said and looked at me, her eyes precisely the same height as mine. "I have coffee back at my place."

There have occasionally been nights like that, when I was convinced of what a lucky thing it was that my little brother had absolutely no idea what he was missing.

SEVEN

*W*HEN I FINALLY GET TO THEIR BASE CAMP I FIND Paul waiting outside with his goggles off, standing in the shade of a building, a rifle leaning against the wall beside him.

"Just in case," he says.

"Thanks," I say. But he doesn't speak much. Instead he picks up the gun and walks away.

I follow him around to the main building. There are three in total, painted white. I guess that was to camouflage them from old 1980s Russian planes in preparation for a nuclear attack that never came. They look at least sixty years old and I wonder if, in taking down the radar towers, the teams are also going to dismantle the buildings themselves. Seems like a waste of resources. What's wrong with three abandoned buildings up near the ceiling of the world where they might, one day, do some good for some lonely hiker? I ask Paul about this.

"They're leaking lead into the ground," he says. "Cheap, post-war concrete."

And I have to agree with him that this is probably answer enough.

We pass a couple of towers that don't have radar dishes atop them and I want to ask what they're for but I figure I'm not going to get much of an answer. Paul does deign to point out the landing strip to our right. "We have to keep it clear in case of emergency. No snow for thirty-three days though."

I look around but I don't see any plane. How did these people get here? I ask Paul but he just grunts and nods vaguely southward.

I keep following him. I think back over my time in the Arctic and realize that I haven't seen a single snowflake fall from the sky so far. I know it's a northern desert with virtually zero precipitation, but it's still strange when I consider that there are these endless fields of ice around me and probably not enough packing snow to make one snowman.

The building Paul leads me to turns out to be a combination kitchen/mess hall/common area. There's an ancient television sitting dusty in the corner. Four people—each as dusty as the television but each of them certainly younger than me—are playing euchre around a long, rectangular table.

Cecilia stands up and introduces me to the three I haven't met yet. They're all white, bearded boys, who could have been from any random small town in Ontario. Turns out I'm exactly right.

"Tom Ullrich, he's from Uxbridge."

"Hey."

"Terry Partridge from Welland."

"Hey."

"And Bryan Coghlin from Richmond."

Bryan gets up from the table, walks over and gives me a hug. "Nice to meet you," he says and I wonder how long it's been since these people have had showers and then, just as it hit me a few hours earlier about my hair, I wonder what the hell a month without a shower must smell like. I make a note not to sit too close to anyone.

"I'm Charles Perth," I say for the second time that day, and watch their eyes carefully for a reaction. There isn't one. "How long have you all been up here?" I ask.

"Going on three months now," says Bryan.

"Don't you guys listen to the news, the radio or anything? Surely you have the Internet up here."

"Yeah...we have all that stuff," says Terry Partridge from Welland, "but no one's really interested in it."

"Oh," I say.

"So what are you doing up here?" asks Bryan, and I realize that he's not-too-subtly checking me out.

"Well, I'm walking to Russia, I guess. It's, you know, been on the news a bit and stuff."

"And what are you going to do when you get there? You think the Russians are going to let you walk into their country without going through customs?"

"They're expecting me."

"They're expecting some Canadian dude to walk across the Arctic Circle? You phoned ahead? Got a Russian pizza waiting for you on the other side?" He's teasing me a bit, but I can tell he's being friendly.

"I phoned ahead, yeah."

"So no passport needed if you call ahead?"

"I've got dual citizenship. They allow that now."

"Hm," he says, and goes back to his card game.

I take a seat beside them and offer to play the winner. I haven't played euchre in six or seven years, but it's not a hard game to pick up on the fly. Eventually the promised scotch makes an appearance and the game changes to poker—the loser has to clear the air strip in the morning. At some point either Terry or Tom goes to the kitchen and makes stew for everyone and I find that Cecilia was wrong about one thing: the food I've been eating along the way is a *lot* better than the stuff they have to suffer with. We stay up talking and drinking and trading stories about the Arctic for hours and hours. It occasionally occurs to me to wonder who's in charge of this operation, but it seems impolitic to ask.

There are only six of us but the personalities fill the room to capacity. Eventually Paul goes to bed with a few mumbled words and once he's gone Cecilia offers to show me the radar towers.

"It'll be worth it," she says. And, with the scotch giving me an irrational sense of self-worth, I eagerly follow her.

It feels so much like night that, once outside, I realize I had managed to forget about the sun for a few hours. For the first time in a while, I think: It's not so bad. Because, for the first time in a while, I'm drunk.

My shadow behind me is laughably long. I create what certainly has to be the largest shadow-puppet in the world at that very second.

In the distance I hear the wind wail or howl or something in the G above middle C. I'm pretty sure it's the wind.

"What was that?" I ask, but Cecilia is now quite a ways away, expecting me to follow her. She either doesn't hear me or chooses not to.

She leads me to a tower I hadn't noticed before, painted white like the others but farther away than the four main ones. It has a ladder going straight up that she immediately starts to ascend. Some sober part of my mind tells me to check my right glove to make sure my flesh isn't poking through before I grab the rungs of a metal ladder in sub-zero temperature. The pink tape has been holding up okay, though at this time of day and with this much scotch in me pretty much everything looks pink.

When I get to the top there's a little windowed shelter just big enough for two people and Cecilia's fiddling with some decades-old dials.

I look out and around and feel that conflict inside myself for wanting to hate anything and everything to do with the Arctic and, at the same time, to admit that it's all so wonderfully beautiful. I gaze toward what I think is north and try to picture myself there somewhere, way beyond the curve of the horizon, up at the top of it all. That little piece of ice on which you can stand and have the entire globe spin around beneath you. Stand still for twenty-four hours and the world under your feet will simply turn you gently counter-clockwise to see the entire universe. Earth as your own personal merry-go-round.

I look at the nearer distances and I hate it all over again.

"How can you guys stand it up here for three months straight? What do you do with all your time?"

Cecilia finishes fiddling and grabs a kind of periscope-type thing hanging from the ceiling, puts the eyepiece up to her face. "Well, it's like we don't listen to the radio or check any messages from back home, you know? It's too nice up here. We like it. We're not in a rush to go back, and we don't want to ruin it with talking to people from anywhere south of seventy-five." And I think, momentarily: I'm from south of seventy-five degrees. But then she pulls my head over to hers and motions for me to emulate her. "Here," she says. "Look."

Look...

I put the eyepiece up against my face, worried that it's going to freeze there permanently, and I see the most beautiful thing I've seen in, well...the most beautiful thing I've seen in a while, anyway. Darkness.

Through the periscope-thing I can see, as clear as the Arctic air, a sky as dark as night. And stars, too. Glorious, wonderful stars.

"Oh," I say, and just keep looking and looking and looking. When I eventually pull myself away I find that Cecilia's no longer up in the tower with me. Reluctantly I climb down and find her waiting at the bottom.

"That was wonderful," I say, as I lower my goggles onto my eyes and everything becomes slightly dimmer again.

"Yeah," she says. "It's pretty neat. Bryan found it. It's not real, it's just a reconstruction put together by the radar towers, but still."

"Radar towers can detect visible light?"

"What the hell do I know?" she asks, and I admit to myself that I'm not entirely sure. She starts to walk, not exactly in a straight line, back toward the mess hall. I follow her, a few paces behind. When we get near, in the broad daylight of something like three o'clock in the morning, I take hold of her sleeve and pull her around the side of the building. I press her up against the wall and try to kiss her, but she pushes me away, laughing crystal-clear in G-sharp.

"Paul would kill you," she says.

"Oh," I say. "I had no idea." And I think to myself that, yeah, she's probably right.

We walk back to the mess hall but by that time everyone's left, so Cecilia leads me to the bunk house.

"Any one that's not taken," she says. There are only about twelve bunks; clearly the base wasn't meant to accommodate a huge military force.

I find an empty bunk in the darkness of a room where the windows are covered in black garbage bags. I fall asleep with images of the beautiful night sky spinning around me.

Look...

In the morning I find I'm awake before everyone else. This is unusual back at home so, for the first time in weeks, I check the time on the GPS that I slept with all night in my pocket—I've found it hard to sleep if it's out of my reach—and realize that a whole day has passed and that it is in fact "night" again. Just past midnight.

I walk down to the bathroom and ascertain that they do have showers after all. In my inebriation of the night before I hadn't noticed. I didn't bring a towel with me and none seem available, but now that the option has presented itself there is nothing in the world I want more than a shower. I reach into one of the stalls and test the water and discover that somehow, even this far north, they have hot water in the pipes.

I strip down to nothing and climb in and take the greatest shower any human being has ever taken since we climbed down out of the trees. My skin had forgotten what it was like to simply be *wet* with something other than sweat, never mind being *clean*.

Afterward I slowly walk back to my bunk and take my time pulling my clothes on, trying not to wake anyone. I discover then that someone during the course of the previous day had repaired my glove. I look at the five sleeping bodies around me but I can barely tell one from the other.

"Thanks," I whisper to all of them.

It seems like a good idea to crawl back in bed but I'm not tired any more. It never occurred to me, when I was packing, to bring a book or anything with me. I didn't think I'd have a single second of free time. If I wasn't busy walking or eating or setting the tent or striking the tent or sleeping, well...well, now it's hard to see how people fill their lives with anything *but* those five things, though I have a vague recollection of what it was like to sit on a bench by the boardwalk.

The only pastime I brought with me is the harmonica, and I haven't had much of a chance to use it so far. I hadn't known when I packed it but harmonicas *suck* in sub-zero weather. The moisture gets into the holes and freezes and there is absolutely nothing you can do to clear them without thawing it out completely. After one night during my first week up here, trying to play in my tent for company, I realized it was pointless. It would freeze even there. I suppose I could play with my head actually *in* my sleeping bag, but not only would I run out of air pretty quickly (my equipment, for all its warmth and durability, sure doesn't breathe well), but the sound would be intolerably shallow.

I go to the empty mess hall and pull a chair into a corner, and for almost an hour I fill the room with the most haunting music I can summon from my tiny little instrument. Eventually I get tired again and find my way back to bed.

In the real morning I pack up my stuff, grab a quick bite of breakfast, then let them know I'm going to be on my way.

"That was fast," says Terry around a mouthful of toasted bagel.

"Yeah, well, I'm on a kind of a schedule," I say. "I have a thing I gotta do."

They walk me outside, then stand around, not really sure what to say; these are five people who don't get a lot of visitors. I thank them individually for their hospitality and mention I am grateful to whoever fixed my glove. At first I had thought it was Cecilia, but now I'm pretty sure it was Bryan Coghlin from Richmond.

"If you get in trouble just, you know, head on back," says Cecilia, and I wonder if she could actually be drunk at eight o'clock in the morning. I decide that's entirely possible.

"Thanks," I say, nodding to them all collectively, and then I turn to leave.

From behind me, Paul McCartney says to be careful but I don't acknowledge it. Instead I just keep walking.

It is far, far too late in the day for advice like that.

EIGHT

$\mathcal{I}$T WAS THE END OF AUTUMN. THE END OF AUTUMN always reminded me of when my parents would take me out of class and ship me off to music camp for a week. Some of the most memorable weeks of my life.

At camp I quickly realized that people with perfect pitch were few and far between. Until then I hadn't known that not everyone possessed the ability—in fact, the involuntary compulsion—to know the precise note of a car horn or cricket chirp or *ting* of a subway token falling into the payment box. For a long time I thought everyone could do this. I thought everyone *had* to do it. I didn't know that for most people it was an impossibility. For me it was like finding out that while people could perceive colours, and might recognize that a bunch of balloons were distinct from each other, almost everyone was unable to name what the colours were. Like looking at the sun and the sky and going: all right, I can tell that they're different colours, but I can't tell you if they're blue and yellow or green and red.

Once I started going to music camp I realized I was quite rare indeed. Turns out that perfect pitch—absolute pitch, whatever—only occurs in about one in every 10,000 people. That meant the chances were that I was the only kid in my high school who could tell you that Ms. Muir, the librarian, tended to shush people in a very insistent middle G.

In my own family my ability went largely unrecognized. Sure, the whole family knew I was a great piano player, but so was my mom and so were three of my cousins. Big deal. My parents had another son who, while he had problems getting along with other people, could do university-level math when he was only seven. While I was at summer music camps in my later childhood, Larry went to math camp. After it seemed that a "camp" type of environment was irreconcilable with Larry's disability (which wasn't even diagnosed until he was nine), he spent a few summers in an Asperger's treatment program. This wasn't meant to "cure" him, but to allow him to interact more "normally" with others. He didn't like it and eventually he refused to go. My mom, after doing some research on family-support websites for parents of kids with Asperger Syndrome, eventually sided with him.

Her son was *not* disabled, she would tell people. He was simply *different*. There was no need to see him as any less of a person than the rest of us just because his brain was focused more on maths and sciences than on interpersonal relationships. That didn't make him wrong or bad or "retarded," it simply made him *different*. Thus, there was no reason to insist that he keep going to the treatment program; there was no need to pay attention to the continual hyping of experimental cures for autism or the neurological rebuilding programs going on in China. Her son Lawrence was fine the way he was. If he didn't get along all the time with the rest of society, then that was as much society's fault as it was his.

I saw her point on this. Over the course of human history, it seemed likely that the dudes with some way to focus intently for hours or days upon a single problem and not get bogged down by emotions...Well, I could see how that might have led to amazing discoveries. Maybe the guy who learned how to harness fire had something different going on in his mind. Maybe Copernicus had Asperger's. Or maybe Galileo. If we had some sort of wonderful treatment for them, how much longer might it have taken us to acknowledge that the Earth goes around the sun and not vice versa? If we had systematically rounded up those who were outside of the neurological norm and put them in special schools, where might we be? If the outliers of humanity are the ones with enhanced brain capacity, through no fault of their own, should they not be given every opportunity to benefit human civilization? Even if it meant they had to live in houses by themselves in North York and never have girlfriends?

Other times I strongly (but quietly) disagreed with my mother. Yes, Larry *was* different from everyone else and it *was* simply our judgment criteria that made him out to be less valued as a member of society than the rest of us. Sure. Fine. But Larry simply couldn't get along with most people. He didn't possess empathy for anyone else and, if he was meeting someone new and they didn't know this about him, it was ninety percent of the time going to start off on the wrong foot. If there were ways to make that easier for my little brother, tricks or shortcuts or something that could substitute for real social skills, then I thought he should have them.

After all, the rest of us can use calculators if we want to do complex math problems. Why shouldn't we give Larry a little help when he needed it too?

It was the end of autumn and I had decided to visit him again. Constant communication with Sandra had made me feel closer to him and, with our mother gone, I guess I felt a little more responsible for Larry than I used to. Most days it was hard for me to acknowledge that he was dying, and I knew that had a lot to do with my wanting us to be closer. No one wants their little brother to die mad at them.

We were standing in Larry's blackboard office because he had wanted to show me something, but by the time we reached the second floor he had forgotten what.

"So...how's the search going?" I asked, knowing as I said it that I'd have to be more specific. Larry stared at me blankly, as though I had asked him what colour of purple he had eaten for lunch that day. "The search for an Internet girlfriend, I mean."

"Oh, right. Yes. It's going along, you know."

"Meet anyone interesting so far?"

Larry doesn't blush. What he does instead is get confused. He's unable to identify and interpret what he feels when he gets embarrassed, so he finds himself the nearest seat and puts his hands on his knees.

I went over and sat beside him.

"It's okay," I said, making my face open and sincere, smiling so he could tell that I meant him well. "You don't have to tell me. Just, you know, make sure that you're happy."

"Oh," he said and then searched inside himself for a few seconds. "Yes, I'm quite happy. I've been talking to Sandra, you know." Sandra and I had been seeing each other almost every day, so I knew that she was still consulting for him and, from what I could piece together from the little she let slip, Larry's online profile had been getting some attention. "She told me I should do it for cancer."

"Um, she said what?"

"She said the walk. Across the Arctic Circle. I could do it to raise money for cancer. I know it won't cure me, Charlie, it'll be too late, but it would be nice for other people. Billions of dollars maybe. I know a lot of rich people, you know."

And it was true, he really did. Throughout university and in the many jobs he'd had, Larry had met almost everyone worth meeting in the business world. And because Larry was so logical, literal-minded and efficient at work, almost all of them thought fondly of him. It seemed plausible he could raise a few million dollars for cancer, even if he'd never walk across the Arctic Circle. I'd never known him to be careless with numbers but it did sound like he'd said "billions" rather than "millions." I decided to let it slide; he was so happy with the idea of his project.

"Do you remember what you wanted to show me?" I asked. He gave me his blank stare again. I filled in the details: "When I first got here you asked me to follow you upstairs so you could show me something."

"I did?"

"Yes, you did, and then you brought me into this office."

He looked at the objects on the desks around him but nothing seemed to jog his memory. Then he looked at the blackboard where was scrawled a very crude musical staff, in treble clef, no notes written in yet.

"I remember!" he said and left the room, returning just a moment later. "This was Dad's and he never gave it to you and it was in his stuff so I thought you can have it because I can't play it and he brought it back from Russia with him when he was young." He smiled and held out his hand and I looked down at something I hadn't seen in fifteen years. I took it from Larry gratefully and carefully, the nicest thing my brother had ever done for me.

It was our dad's old harmonica.

"You are welcome, Charlie," he said.

And for the second time in decades my brother left me speechless.

NINE

I'T'S EARLY IN MY DAY WHEN I COME ACROSS A SPOOKY, abandoned Inuit trading camp. The long shadows of the habitation stretch off across the northern ice shelf, pointing me in the right direction. I'm not great with telling how old things are, and places like this sure as hell last forever up in the north, where everything takes ten times longer to decompose. So the camp could be 300 years old or it could be thirty. I figure it's almost certainly from that brief period of time when everything was thawed up here but, lacking a stone placed in the side of one of the shacks with the date carved right into it and the name of some long-dead Lieutenant Governor, I'd be doing little more than guessing.

It's been three days since I left the radar detection base behind me. So far I've managed to reach all the food caches no problem. None have contained any messages from my brother. I've been skirting the northwest coast of Ellesmere Island and now I'm right at the tip, according to the GPS. I was going to spend the night here but now I think I'd rather keep going. Building a fire with the lumber from the buildings would be nice, and probably my last opportunity, but I don't want to hang around longer than I have to. I'll be leaving land behind me today and it's going to take about two weeks to get to the Pole, but a total of forty-five or fifty days until I reach Russia on the other side. First stop Tiksi, then onward through the country to Verkhoyansk. From there it's a short walk down to the border of the Arctic Circle on the other side of the world. There'll be a clay road to walk on. Hell, there'll be taverns in which I can buy beer. But that's all quite a ways away. Today I'm saying goodbye to Canada and preparing to travel to the land of my father.

He's been on my mind for the past two days. I can hear his voice in the wind sometimes. He's been dead for fifteen years and I'm trying to recount pieces of advice that he must surely have provided me over the years. Instead, all I'm getting are random facts formed in *Jeopardy!*-ese.

Eight.

He liked hockey and travel. He was into politics even though—or maybe because—for most of his time in Canada he wasn't able to vote. He changed his name to Perth when he arrived here. He loved his wife and his two sons. And, like any self-respecting Russian, he enjoyed his vodka. But in addition to all this, he loved *Jeopardy!*. Especially re-runs with the old Canadian host, Alex Trebek. It didn't make a lot of sense, his fascination with the show. It wasn't like he ever got any of the questions right unless they were about Russian politics, Russian geography or Russian history. Even if the category was sports and the answer was some Russian gymnast or something, he usually wouldn't get it.

*What is the number of toes that Robert Peary had amputated
during his Arctic expeditions between 1886 and 1909?*

I wonder what my father would make of this place.

The little trading huts still stand askew on the coast, built mainly of driftwood but also of logs that must have been shipped for thousands of kilometres from the Yukon. Or maybe even further, maybe Alaska or B.C. Most of the site is a complete wreck. You can tell what used to be living quarters and what used to be a smoking hut and what had been a storage shack to keep the pelts safe from curious predators. Polar bears used to thrive on this coast before the world heated up and they came near to extinction. Now with the water frozen all year round they've had to move far south where seals and fish remain plentiful. It's kind of ironic, really.

I walk over to the largest hut that's still standing and give one of the beams a good shove. It doesn't fall over so I put the goggles on my forehead, take a chance and enter. Inside it's a little bigger than a mini-van. When I get up close it smells like ancient, untreated wood and feces. Some animals have been using it for shelter. There are bones on the floor. Fish, or maybe Arctic hare.

There's a pot hanging from the wall. I take it down and notice a hole has been burned straight through the bottom. I wonder briefly how much it would fetch on eBay. I turn to leave but am startled by a small movement in the corner of the shack. I lift my hand, hoping to be threatening, and see a corresponding movement. My reflection. There's most of a broken but still perfectly clear mirror hanging from a hook on the back wall.

I take it outside, amazed that it hasn't oxidized after all this time.

I sit down on the frozen coast, sun to my back, and take a look at myself, unable to decide what it is that I see. It's either me, a lot older than I've ever known myself, or my father, a lot younger than I remember him.

1968.

Ever since I started this journey I've had doubts about how the idea got started. The initial idea, I mean. I told Larry that our dad once expressed a desire to walk from Canada to Russia across the Arctic Circle, but I'm no longer sure that was the case. I think I remember him saying something like that, but now I think that he maybe only wanted to cross the Bering Strait. Through the Yukon, through Alaska and then just eighty-five kilometres to Russia. A two-day walk across open ice.

What is the year of the first undisputed land journey to the North Pole, Alex?

I lean back on my hands and look forward across the treeless, featureless expanse of ice. A fifty-day journey until I see land again.

Those food caches had damn well better be there.

I walk over to the ruins of the smoking hut, where fish and whale meat would have been preserved during the warmer months, and I sit down to change my shoes. The steel-cleated boots I'd been wearing up to this point have served me well, but it's time to put on real snowshoes. Well, not "real" snowshoes. Not tennis-racket-shaped contraptions made of maple, leather and rawhide. These are lightweight, titanium numbers, foldable, and they look more like shiny, complicated mouse-traps than tennis rackets.

I take a short walk around the camp to get used to the new foot-wear. It's nice to have my pack off and I find that I'm not at all looking forward to setting foot on open ocean. I walk out a ways to test the shoes. They seem okay and I find that it's much easier to walk without the pack on. I could probably do an extra ten or fifteen kilometres per day. The snowshoes give me a freedom that I hadn't had before. For the first time in a long time, I'm actually kind of enjoying myself. I go out twenty, thirty metres onto the pack ice and notice that I'm holding the broken mirror.

My dad would have loved this kind of thing.

Murmansk, population 350,000.

Jeopardy! That old Canadian host, before the one they have on there now. Alex Trebek. He was never the same after he shaved his mous-tache. I remember seeing old send-ups they did of the show on *Satur-day Night Live* back in the nineties, sketches about *Celebrity Jeopardy!* And I think: that's what I'm doing now. That's what this whole damn journey is about. It's one long, looong version of *Celebrity Jeopardy!* Am I going to see one cent once this thing is done? Once I'm safely in Russia, in some Russian hotel somewhere, drinking vodka, maybe being asked questions in broken English by some small Russian media outlet, am I going to be any richer for the journey? Everyone got to see me on national news when I came forward and announced the trek, but once it's finished I'm certainly not going to get any money from it. I get to donate it all to "the charity of my choice," in this case some sort of multi-directional donation coordinated by the Canadian Cancer Society, the Princess Margaret Hospital and a new cancer research foundation they're in the process of setting up at the University of Toronto.

What is the largest city north of the Arctic Circle?
What was my dad's hometown?

Of all the places I've visited in the north I've never been to Murmansk. It's not even a town, really, but a bustling city, bigger than some of Canada's provincial capitals. It's got a larger population than the entire country of Iceland. Maybe when this adventure's over I'll go there. Maybe once I miss the Arctic again. So, like, in twenty or thirty years.

I look at myself in the mirror again, then return it to its hook. On the off chance that it's been there for hundreds of years, it may as well stay there. I'm not going to need it where I'm going. Some poor Inuit schmuck might have traded ten seal pelts to the Hudson's Bay Company for that thing, then fled this place and left it behind.

Maybe, in the end, he thought the broken mirror only brought him bad luck.

I grab my pack and say goodbye to land, goodbye to Canada. I have an impulse to take a small stone with me as a memento of my home country, but I figure I have souvenirs enough already. Instead I build a tiny Inukshuk on the coast. A little stone man to tell people that I was here.

TEN

*I*T WAS WINTER. THE NATIONAL SCIENCE FICTION CON-
vention was in Hamilton and Sandy asked me to go with her.

"It's where I meet a lot of my clients," she said. Which was great for
her, but it still didn't sound like much of a reason for me to go. "I'll be
there," she said. And that was reason enough.

I don't know if there's a real correlation between people with Asperger's or other social maladjustment problems and an affinity for science
fiction, but it certainly seems to me that there is. Larry used to be really
into *Star Trek* and all that kind of stuff and, though I'd read *Dune* and
Lord of the Rings, I didn't know much about the genre.

"What's it going to be like?" I asked. "Just a bunch of nerds sitting
around, talking about nerd movies and books and dressed up in costumes and stuff?"

"You'll see," she said, smiling.

As it turned out, it was just a bunch of nerds sitting around, talking
about nerd movies and books and dressing up in costumes and stuff.

It was a *five-day* affair. Sandy paid for weekend passes for both of
us. On the Friday night we went to a panel talk called "How to Flirt

at Conventions." It was given by four people whom I *really* couldn't imagine had gotten laid at *any* point in their lives—and they were easily in their fifties or older.

"This is one of the most uncomfortable experiences I've ever been through," I whispered halfway through the panel.

"Shhh," she said. She was grinning, having a great time.

Most of the discussion was about how important it is for people to make eye contact, to stand in front of someone when you're talking to them, not to gush over how amazing you think their eyes are when you first meet them. The kind of thing that any normal person would think went without saying but was clearly the kind of thing that people like my brother need spelled out for them. I looked around the room and saw that people were *taking notes.*

I wanted to flee, but Sandy held me to my seat.

When it was almost over, she stood up and made a short announcement about the service she offered, helping people make their online dating-site profiles more attractive and interesting to members of the opposite sex. I knew most of the guys in the room were only half-listening to what she was saying. She had dressed in a low-cut top and a classy, medium-length skirt. Her hair was down and her makeup was perfect. She said she'd leave her business cards at the front for people to take on their way out and I don't think there was a single guy who left that room—not even the panellists—without picking one up.

"Smooth," I said when we were back in the hallway. She nodded, a job well done.

"Sandra!" called someone from down the hall, some tall, goateed fellow in a kilt, advancing toward us and dragging his nerdly consort girl by the hand behind him.

"Kevin," Sandy said. "It's nice to see you."

"You too," he replied, and it seemed as though he was making an incredible effort to look her in the eye when he talked to her. "I wanted you to meet Heather."

"Hi, Heather," said Sandy. "And this is Charlie."

"Hi," I said, feeling like some kind of mundane alien from planet *The Real World*.

"Heather, this is the woman who helped me with my profile."

"Oh!" said Heather, and then her face lit up. She probably hadn't known what to make of Sandy before that. "It's really great to meet you. Thanks so much. I know Kevin can be kind of a doofus, and I don't think we woulda met without you, you know? He's getting better though." She playfully elbowed her boyfriend in the ribs.

"Anyway," said Kevin, adjusting his nerd kilt, "we're on our way to a talk but I wanted to say hi. And thanks."

"No problem, you guys. Really. I wish you all the best together." Sandy handed each of them one of her cards, in case they knew of people who could use her services.

"Thanks," they both said, fit to burst with joy for the wonderfulness of life and Gene Roddenberry, and then they walked away, hand in hand, to hear some talk about the physics of fictional warp drive ships or something equally awesome.

"So that's what you do," I said, only marvelling at her a little bit. "You help people."

"Yeah," she said.

"Huh." And we left to spend the rest of the night alone in our room.

On the morning of the second day we went to a reading by some famous author I'd never heard of and Sandy "networked" with a few people who—they were the first to admit—really could benefit from her services. It seemed that she got a lot of business by word of mouth. Once she introduced herself to people it was hard for them not to point her out in the crowds, say that they knew her, tell their friends about what she does, how she can help. Also, she was a woman who was quite noticeably *not* dressed up in a Princess Leia costume, and she was also quite noticeably the most head-turning woman there. When she walked by, everyone set their phasers to stunned. And being one of the only normal- and athletic-looking guys at the convention, I really didn't mind at all.

We had lunch in the cafeteria on Saturday and sat beside a table of three guys who reminded me of nothing so much as Larry, ten years younger.

"So how's my little brother doing?" I asked.

"What do you mean?" she asked around a mouthful of convention-centre poutine.

"What's your professional opinion? Think there's any hope for him?"

"Well, it's really hard to say. I mean, I go online as him once in a while, so I know his profile has been getting an uptick of interest lately, but I don't think he's been on a single date yet. Or, if he has, he's very reluctant to talk about it."

"Yeah, he's like that. You have to leave him alone and he'll figure things out. Well, not that kind of thing I guess. Usually math problems, logic problems. Like this Arctic Circle trip thing he's got planned."

"Yeah, what's up with that?"

"The Arctic?"

"Yeah. I mean, sure, he's dying. We all are. But he *knows* his time is limited...but why the Arctic Circle? Couldn't he have been the first to do something else?"

"Like what?"

"I don't know, like...well, I don't know."

I reached for the vinegar and protected my onion rings with it. Sandra didn't like vinegar but she did like onion rings. "When we were younger, our parents would take us all around the northern part of the world. Our dad was from pretty much as north in Russia as you could get and I guess he just missed it. While all our friends were going to Florida and the Caribbean for March break, we'd be going to Lapland. So I guess it just grew on us.

"I remember the first time we went to Whitehorse in the winter. There wasn't a single day warmer than minus thirty degrees Celsius. We were staying at a hotel down by the water and most of the city was shut down because it was winter holidays. All the shops were supposed to open up again after the New Year, but we would have left for Dawson by then.

"Larry and I were still in high school and I remember I had wanted to spend the New Year doing something a hell of a lot more fun than having dinner with my parents. My dad had had a few vodkas early in the night, so I managed to convince him to let me take a walk around the town. He seemed to think this was a fine idea, but I had to take Larry with me, right? Whitehorse might seem relatively north, but it's still about five hundred kilometres to the Arctic Circle. It has daylight throughout the winter, but the nights are dark and long. And White-horse is just like any other North American city after dark, so not the safest place to be if you're a teenager from out of town. That said, it does have one thing going for it: people do *not* hang out on the streets in the winter. At minus thirty-five and lower it doesn't take long for the homeless to make their way to shelters."

"Your parents sound like they were pretty fun," she said and made a face as she took a bite of one of my rings.

"Well, yeah. They were all right. Anyway, I dragged my brother into the dark and down to the Yukon river through the fog."

"It's foggy up there?"

I looked at her as I would at someone who had never really tasted fine scotch before. She was missing out on a whole wonderful part of the world and didn't even know it.

"Ice fog," I said, nodding.

"Ice fog?"

"Ice fog, Sandra. It's something. It's really one of the strangest things you can find in the northern parts of the world. Maybe anywhere. You might be at sea level, the temperature might be minus forty degrees, but you can barely see three metres in front of you because of the tiny crystals of ice floating in mid-air. It looks like regular fog but *much* harder to see through, and much more improbable. I don't know why the crystals don't fall to the ground. I guess it's like clouds way up in the atmosphere on a cold winter's day. You know there's *no way* there can actually be water vapour at that altitude, but they don't fall to the ground. It's like that, except right in front of your face and smarter people on the streets of Whitehorse take to walking with flashlights so they don't get hit by cars. Drivers can barely see the road in front of them, even in the daylight."

"Ice fog."

I smile and nod, grabbing a retaliatory scoop of her poutine. "Anyway, so we go down to the river and just sit there, watch the steam come up off of it."

"*Steam?*"

"Well, it's minus thirty-five and the water is obviously a little bit above zero; it doesn't freeze until March some years. So, yeah. Ice steam. At night it's wild, with the lights from the town shining off it. We go to the river and throw stones in—Larry was always a better stone skipper than me—and five or six town kids eventually walked down there too and I figured we should probably leave, but they're wasted and friendly. They come over and one of the girls asks our names and I tell her and then she does something weird; she asks for our *last* names. I still remember that. Like when, in Toronto, as a teenager, if you were meeting someone new, would you ever ask for their *last* name?

"Anyway. So I tell her, and she says: you must know my sister. At first I think: who the hell is her sister, and why is she so notorious that two kids from Toronto should have heard of her? But then it dawns on me that this chick assumes we're from there, that she simply doesn't recognize us and, if *she* doesn't know who we are then *surely* her sister would. It's just such a small town, you know?

"Anyway, so we're standing around for a while and we say we're from Toronto and we're talking about the ice fog and what it's like to live up there and I guess it's getting kinda late and I know we should get back to our parents. Our dad wouldn't care but I knew our mom would be worried.

"When we're saying goodbye this girl—I don't remember her name, but I'd bet a thousand bucks that Lar does—she goes up to him and she kisses him on the cheek. You know, he's not a really bad-looking guy, especially if he's wearing a toque, and if you've only been talking to him for a couple of minutes, and you're drunk off your face, maybe he seems okay. It was only a Happy New Year's kiss, harmless fun for her. Some strange boy from out of town, you know?

"Yeah. So that was the first time a girl ever kissed him. In minus-thirty-five degree weather, ice fog all around us, New Year's Eve on the waterfront in Whitehorse.

"He's been drawn to the north and the Arctic ever since. I used to kid him because he loved that cold and winter and stuff so much. Growing up, I used to joke that he had Iceberger Syndrome. He liked that and then he'd sometimes say it too, but of course he doesn't really understand what a pun is."

"Iceberger Syndrome."

"Yeah."

"That's funny," she said.

"Yeah, kinda, I guess."

Sandra grabbed the last onion ring off my tray and popped it in her mouth. I gathered up the garbage and we got up to leave. We had to get to a panel discussion on how to make realistic fantasy costumes. Sandra figured there'd be nothing but young men there who could *really* use her help.

"Anyway, I'm sure that if his job had accommodated him he would have moved up to Yellowknife or something a long time ago. But they don't have the kinds of facilities he needs."

"You mean, like, psychiatric facilities?"

"No, I mean, like, labs and libraries and stuff like that. Think tanks with half a dozen other people like him all working individually on projects for the Canadian Space Agency and stuff."

"Charlie, what does Larry *do* exactly?"

"Well, actually, he's kind of like you. He solves problems for people. They're, you know, on an entirely different spectrum. Logic problems."

"Hey! I solve logic problems too, they're just...a different *kind* of logic."

"Yeah," I said. "Maybe you do. Who was it? Mr. Spock? The most logical guy in the universe, he couldn't even crack a smile? Did he ever have a date?"

"Well, if he didn't, I bet I could get him one," she said. And she was so confident and smart and so damned good at her job that I agreed with her. I didn't have any idea what she saw in me but I figured that as long as we kept our dates to weekend-long science fiction conventions, I wouldn't have too difficult a time keeping her by my side.

ELEVEN

$\mathscr{M}$Y THIRD FULL DAY ON THE ICE AND SOMETHING'S following me.

Sleeping in the tent for the past three "nights" has been markedly different from any of the previous ones, even when there had been ice directly below me. There's something about knowing that there isn't any land close by, and none underneath me—just four or five metres of frozen water and then the cold Arctic Ocean all the way to the bottom. If there were a kind of miracle quick thaw and the ice were to open up underneath my tent in the middle of the night, I wouldn't stand a chance.

I noticed something moving quickly on the horizon to the south earlier today. It's hard not to notice something like that when you're surrounded by nothing but a flat, shelter-less field of ice for hundreds of kilometres. I was still about five klicks away from the next food cache and happened to glance back and there it was: something. Something indistinct, but something for sure.

I look back now and see that it's still there, something making a crude bump on the horizon right on the same route I've been taking, and I *know* that I didn't pass any crude bumps in the past forty-eight hours. This thing is coming for me and it's moving slowly but not stopping and, really, against all probability, there's only one thing it can be. I pick up my pace, which I should have been doing anyway but the added motivation—unwelcome though it is—encourages me. I'm getting hungry by this point in the day but I've been trying to avoid walking faster than I'm comfortable with. There's nothing worse than sweating through your innerwear when it's minus twenty.

I lie. There are a million things worse than that. One of which happens to be on my mind presently.

I take a mental inventory of every piece of equipment I've got on my back, but the best and only weapon I have with me is my pick-axe and, while I'm sure it's strong enough to be a threat to probably any animal on the planet, I have a feeling that an adult polar bear wouldn't let me get close enough to use it. I wish I'd spent more time researching and less time working out to prepare for this journey.

What can I do? I keep walking.

It's late in the day so the sun is to my left, my white shadow stretching off to the east, an east with no end point. If I walked due east for a few weeks I would end up right where I am right now. Maybe if I explained something like that to the polar bear, it would have a good long think about it and I could make my escape.

I look back and it's impossible to tell for sure, but I don't think it's gaining on me. It's easier to spot now that its shadow, too, is stretching off to the east. Either that or it actually *is* gaining on me. I turn around and keep walking. If I'm going to keep this pace up I need to find that food cache. I'm sure I can eat while I'm walking.

How is it tracking me? Are polar bear eyes as good as human eyes? It seems unlikely. Can it really smell me from that far away? I hope not. Maybe it's just smart enough to follow the little pinpricks that my snowshoes leave in the ice. Or, hell, maybe it's trying to be the first polar bear to walk from one side of the Arctic Circle to the next. Raising money for climate change or polar bear cancer or something.

I look down at my GPS and I should only be two-point-seven klicks from the food cache. Food would be great. Hot stew. Steak and potatoes. Hell, at this point I'll even take garlic bread. Whatever the organizers damn well wanted to give me.

Polar bears live all over the Arctic, except for Scandinavia. Russia, Greenland, Canada, they've all got them. Iceland doesn't, but that's only because Iceland is a volcanic island with only one indigenous land mammal, the Arctic fox. Yes, there are mice there too, but they were introduced by man. The Icelandic horse, too, direct descendant from its ancient Norse ancestors: once it leaves Iceland—say, to compete in a horse show or something—it's illegal to return it to its native land. But Iceland does not have polar bears. Once in a while, say, a couple of times a decade or so, a polar bear will get caught on an ice floe and drift across. They don't last long, though. Icelandic farmers are rather protective of their sheep.

How the hell long has it been following me? Is it the same one whose tracks I saw over a week ago, before I spent the night at the radar station? It's gotta be. Polar bears are endangered and rare enough in the wild. Once you get this far north you might as well be chased by a sasquatch. Or an abominable snowman.

Thinking of monsters, I realize suddenly that I'm Frankenstein's and I laugh. I've often wondered about how that story ends, with the doctor on a dogsled, chasing his creation across the Arctic, a fight to the death (if you can kill a re-animated corpse) in the North Pole. But then that would make this polar bear Victor Frankenstein and somehow I don't think it's smart enough to dig through graves, unearthing people and stitching them back together.

The GPS says I've got half a kilometre to go. I'm going to have to keep my eyes open. If it's one of the oddly-shaped ones, the ones with postcards in them from my brother, they're easy to miss.

And then I see it. It is one of the ones from my brother, or so I assume. However the hell he's been managing to pull this trick off from his hospital bed down on University Avenue in Toronto I still don't know. I tear it open, the latches twanging in the key of F. The postcard is from Tahiti and it's nothing but a bright blue ocean, a white sandy beach and tropical mountains in the background. The text exclaims *"Beautiful TAHITI!"* My brother's awful handwriting covers the back.

> *Dear Charlie,*
>
> *The media are saying that you're on the ocean now, that you've left our home and native land for the ice shelf. I'm surprised you've made it this far. You should turn back. It will be harder for you from now on.*
>
> *Enjoy your meal.*
> *Lawrence*

No word about my supposedly burned-down home. I look in the cache since I'm eager to grab some food and keep going, but all that's inside is eight cans of processed meat in stylized heating containers. I rip one open and realize that, while it's not Spam exactly, it's a hell of a lot like it, but lower quality if that's possible. I want to vomit.

Larry knows that I can't eat Spam. It's made me puke ever since we were kids, while it's always been one of his favourite meals.

I'm starving, but can I stomach it? I'm not sure.

I look back across the ice at Victor and see that he is a *lot* closer than I'd been expecting. Far closer than I'm comfortable with. Maybe he picked up his pace once he saw me stop, or maybe he caught the smell of the meat and decided he couldn't wait any longer.

I'm starving but I would rather not eat food than be food, and this is the only chance I can see I've got. I remove all eight rectangular cans and turn on their heating units, lay them on the ice and watch them slowly sink, not too deep, but deeper than is immediately convenient. I back away about fifty metres and find that even I can smell them. It doesn't take long for Victor to get there. I pull out my GPS and keep walking backwards.

Charles Perth.

I wonder briefly if processed meat could be at all harmful or poisonous to polar bears, but I see no reason for it. Polar bears can probably eat anything that we eat; and they can eat us, too, just as we can eat them. Polar bear liver is poisonous—Inuit hunters throw it in the ocean so that their dogs don't dig it up and eat it—but the meat and the rest of the organs are fine. After leaving the meat for the bear I realize I should probably have taken a single can for myself. It may be one of my most-hated foods but it's still better than going for a day with nothing at all. And I briefly regret my inability to enjoy a fresh polar bear steak anytime soon.

Who was the first person to walk backwards all the way to the North Pole?

Even from a distance I can see that Victor is thinner than any bear should ever be, never mind a polar bear, animals that only survive up here because of the layers of fat just below their skin. I feel intense sorrow for it and, if I had the means, I would consider putting it out of its misery.

That would be infinitely preferable to it putting me out of mine.

I see that it's probably not an adult. Maybe its growth has simply been stunted because of a lack of food, but it looks pretty young.

I keep backing away slowly and the bear approaches the sunken cans suspiciously. Then it begins to dig them up, tear them out of the ice and eat them whole. I can hear the crunching of the aluminum in its canines and wonder that the heat isn't burning the inside of its mouth. It's probably too hungry to care.

I keep walking, wondering if I can somehow make myself seem like a threat. I am checking the GPS to make sure I'm headed backward in the right direction when Victor, in the middle of devouring his fifth or sixth can, puts his head in his paws and starts to thrash around. He lunges forward onto the ice like a housecat on a cockroach, and I can see he's in immense pain. Then he screams in a distressingly loud C-sharp.

I get an idea.

Which is good, because he sits up and sees me and starts to run.

Polar bears are *fast*.

I turn around and begin to run too. I haven't run in snowshoes before. It's extremely difficult and I want to drop my pack to speed my escape but if I do and Victor destroys it then I'm as good as dead anyway and I'm fumbling with the GPS and it's impossible to manipulate the buttons through my gloves so I tear them off and shove them in my pocket and keep running and running.

I run across the Arctic and think, how the *hell*, Paul McCartney, was I *supposed* to be more careful?

I run across the Arctic and then I trip over something invisible and land hard on my side.

I flip over on my back and look behind me and Victor is twenty metres away. I fumble with the GPS some more and suddenly it emits this extremely loud and *shrill* sound, alternating between A-sharp, C-Sharp and a high E. It's the alarm. Like, to wake you up in the morning. The stupid, stupid alarm.

Victor is wary now and keeps his distance, but I can tell something's wrong with him anyway. I get up just as he lies down on his stomach, flat on the ice, and I can hear him keening softly. I turn off the alarm.

Again I want to go over to him, put him out of his misery. I see blood flow out of his mouth onto the ice. The sharp, jagged tins, torn open in his teeth, must have cut up his insides pretty badly.

I look down at what I tripped over and find that the invisible something looks remarkably like a food cache. Like the kind that was placed here two months ago, but it's less than two hundred metres from the one with all the Spam. Invisible on my GPS, but here nonetheless. I keep one eye on Victor and tear it open. Inside I find, in addition to the regular energy bars: coffee and protein crackers, pork and beans, mashed potatoes and something that seems like a kind of quiche with spinach. And I know suddenly how my brother's been doing his magic trick. He hasn't sent someone up here to replace the original food caches, he has simply sent a plane up here with new ones and then managed to write over the data streaming to my GPS so that I get directed to his boxes rather than the legitimate ones.

I take all the food I'll need out of the cache and decide I'd better walk a couple more kilometres before I eat it.

Victor's still lying prone and my heart is still racing.

Me: saved by Spam and noise.

As I walk I look back frequently. Victor is lying still on the ice and I know that it's sad. I eat meat every day of my life but I've never personally killed an animal before, never mind an endangered one, one who's alone, like me, at the top of the world.

I keep walking.

TWELVE

*I*T WAS THE MIDDLE OF WINTER. I HAD DECIDED NOT TO take on any new clients until the new year, so I was only treating people I had already been seeing for a few months and who were on their way to some kind of recovery. It was a good job when I could help people. People who wanted to re-learn to play the piano after a stroke, or who had been through a car accident and had some limited brain damage and could no longer carry a tune. I wasn't the best or most renowned music therapist in Canada but I was the best and most renowned in Toronto, and that was good enough to pay the mortgage. I had been visiting Larry on an almost weekly basis, usually the day after Sandy would check in on him. I would always tell her how I thought he was doing, even though she refused to discuss confidential aspects of her client with me. Still, I was getting pretty good at piecing together things about Larry based on what she *wouldn't* say.

After a quick peek in his backyard to confirm that the Inukshuk was still unfinished, I sat down with my brother in his living room, a wood-panelled cathedral that was the size of the entire main floor of my house. I had brought a case of beer with me since I knew he liked it.

"How's it going?" I asked. "With the Arctic trip, I mean. Is it all coming together?" At the time I had no idea how serious he was about it.

He hadn't even said hi to me yet but he got up out of his chair, as was his way, left his untouched beer behind him and made his way to the stairs. It meant, as usual, that I was to follow him.

We went up to one of his offices, the one where I had first met Sandra. Now the floors were covered in northern survival gear: high-tech gloves, a backpack, some sort of foldable snowshoes. The walls were now covered in a kind of cork-board material and this, in turn, was covered in high-resolution maps of the post-climate change Arctic.

"Wow," I said, checking out the detail on one of them. It seemed like I could see every little feature of the land if I just peered hard enough: abandoned Cold War radar bases, centuries-old Inuit trading camps, old ships that had got locked in the ice years ago and might not be free for hundreds more. I peered closer, trying to see if I could find Superman's Fortress of Solitude, and then Larry started talking behind me.

"I can do it in one hundred days I think. I can walk that much. It will be light out all the time and always frozen. Daylight in the summer in the Arctic region. Have people drop off supplies beforehand. Food. Auto-heating cans of protein, spaghetti, garlic bread."

Larry always loved his garlic bread.

"I can do it. I can raise money for cancer like Sandra told me to. It's a good idea, I know a lot of people who are in charge of the corporations, they're good with money, they'll do it if I ask them. Probably they'll want to beat each other, they're very competitive, that's why they're good at their jobs like me, I can do it, make a lot of money for cancer research, for people like mom. What is going on between you and Sandra?"

The question caught me off-guard. Larry would often go on long tangents and it was easy to zone out when he got on a particular kick. Sometimes he wouldn't let a topic drop for ten or fifteen minutes; he would just speak in one continual sentence.

"What do you mean, Larry?" I hadn't known that I was hiding anything from him, but perhaps out of a desire not to let slip that Sandy and I talked about him, I may have been overly careful not to suggest that we were together. A couple. An item. She wore my t-shirts to bed when she slept over. That kind of thing. He stood there, arms crossed, and looked at me over his glasses. He often needed elaboration when someone asked him a question, but he knew that most other people did not.

"We've been seeing each other for a while, Larry. I thought you knew that."

"You can't," he said. "I love her." I wasn't sure I heard him properly, and I asked him to repeat himself. He must have interpreted that as mockery or aggression or something—I could never really tell with Larry—because he yelled, "*I love her!*" and picked up a computer monitor, tore it from its cords, and threw it across the room at me. I dodged it and leapt out into the hallway and he chased me. Over my shoulder I could see something close to murder in his eyes. I ran into another one of his offices and slammed the door behind me. I locked it and shoved a desk up against it.

He started throwing himself against the door from the other side.

"Jesus, Larry, calm down!"

"I knew her first!" he yelled, and his body thudded against the hardwood. "I met her!" *Thud!* "I knew her!" *Thud!* "She was helping me!" *Crack!* And then Larry swore at the top of his lungs. I wondered if he had broken something. He was gone for a few seconds and I was about to open the door to see if he was all right when he started pounding on the door again, with something other than his body. I knew that he was now beyond reason.

I went to the window and looked down. It wasn't a far jump and the snow outside was deep. I tore the screen out and leapt before I could think much about it and walked toward my car. I heard my brother's voice yelling from the window behind me. He was brandishing what looked like some kind of miniature pick-axe.

"I would prefer it if you didn't come to my house any more, Charles! Do not ever call me. Do not call my office! Never message me! I can make you miserable but since you are my brother and since I have less than two years to live and an Arctic Circle to walk across, I will let you be. We are still brothers! Do *not* contact me again."

"Okay, Lar," I said, walking slowly backward, "take it easy!"

"*Go now!*"

I went to my car and drove home.

I respected Larry's wishes and didn't get in touch with him. He had, of course, fired Sandy, so she didn't know what was going on with him either. It had been four weeks since the incident. Sandra and I had been together for about three months by that point and though there hadn't been much talk about the future—futures either single or joint—it seemed all right to assume that we were headed in some sort of mutual-future direction.

It was a Monday night and we were at my house watching the evening news. It was about the only thing we watched together and usually one of us would make dinner and we'd sit on the couch and eat and make fun of politicians or drunks who had driven their snowmobiles out into the middle of Lake Simcoe and never returned. After that I would usually practice a new piece on the piano while Sandy got some work done online, or else I would put on some jazz and we'd have some wine and talk. It was a pretty great life and I didn't particularly miss my brother. It was a cruel thing to think, and I knew I'd miss him once he was gone, but a part of me knew I'd be relieved too.

Only a few months to go, I figured.

I had made dinner that night and we were settling in to eat and watch a half hour of political and personal mishaps. Right off the top, though, the night encountered an invincible threat to its relaxingness. The feature on that Monday night's newscast was some holiday feel-good story about a guy from Toronto who had managed to raise a record-setting amount of money for cancer research. Some guy from Toronto who had gotten most of the five hundred biggest multinational corporations to commit themselves enormously, and all he had to do in return was to walk across the Arctic Circle, alone, from Canada to Russia.

I damn near choked on my mushroom casserole.

"*What?*" asked Sandra.

"I don't know," I replied. And I did *not* know *what*.

The news went to commercials and we sat through them in silence. We didn't hold hands, we didn't eat. I might not have even been breathing.

When they came back from commercials the newscaster was saying something wonderful while a picture of my awkwardly smiling brother was displayed in the top-right corner.

"Oh my god," said Sandra. I didn't say anything.

They showed a brief clip of Larry behind a podium, looking stressed as he delivered a statement to the press. Then they went back to the anchor and the photograph of my brother. All I could think for half a minute was: how much time did it take to get that single five-second clip?

It was the biggest combined donation not just to cancer, but to *anything,* in the history of the world. The sum total that Larry had managed to get the corporations to commit was equal to the amount donated to cancer-related causes and international foundations over the previous *nine years.* And all he had to do was walk across the Arctic Circle. Briefly I wondered how much the record-setting donations had to do with Larry's friends thinking he wouldn't be able to do it, but I'm sure that only played a minor role. The initial details were vague, but the reports were all quoting some number *in excess* of two hundred billion dollars.

It was unbelievable. Like, it was really, really hard to believe. I couldn't get in touch with my brother to confirm any of the details, and he wouldn't return my calls, so I was limited to the same news sources as everyone else. It seemed that he was really going to do it. My crazy, Iceberger Syndrome brother was going to walk across the Arctic Circle and he was going to raise billions of dollars—200 billion—for cancer research.

But three weeks later, near the end of winter, the world economy crashed and the corporations *really* did *not* want to have to meet their financial promises. A week after that and the newscasts reported that Larry's cancer had taken a significant turn for the worse. He was forced to stay in the hospital and it looked like the corporations wouldn't have to pay up after all.

THIRTEEN

*I*T'S BEEN NINE DAYS SINCE THE POLAR BEAR AND SLEEP-ing on the ice hasn't gotten any easier. Eating has, though. Ever since I figured out that any time I find one of my brother's caches there will be a corresponding original one with *real,* edible, fortified food somewhere close by, I'm rarely going hungry. His spiteful notes are even kind of motivating. Since he's not very good at recognizing what gets under his own skin, he's not very good at saying things that hurt other people.

I still wonder about my house, though.

Less than fifty centimetres.

For the past four days it has been nothing but monotony. Today I've begun watching the GPS and counting how many steps I take per kilometre and then trying to beat the previous record by no more than a single step. I'm not trying to overstretch myself, it's just a game.

What is the average annual amount of precipitation at the North Pole?

I put one foot in front of the other and am grateful that my boots inside the snowshoes don't give me blisters. It's one thing to walk for a hundred days straight across the scalp of the planet, it would be quite another if I had to do it with sore feet.

I really wish I had brought something to read with me. Just one book. Even if I had to read it a thousand times. Or even some kind of listening device, connected to a satellite relay that could read books to me.

I put one foot in front of the other, grateful that it's not colder out today than I had expected. Usually it's only about minus twenty, which is about the same as a relatively cold winter day in Toronto. Uncomfortable if you're not dressed for it, but bearable if you're prepared. If you keep moving.

And what do I have to do if not keep moving?

Who tries to walk to the North Pole on their own? With no one else to talk to, no one to complain about the cold with? No one to save them from polar bears? This idea of Larry's, of mine, of my father's, was flawed right from the start. There's a reason no one's ever walked across the Arctic Circle before, and a reason that people don't take random hikes to the North Pole by themselves: it's lonesome.

In 1995 Richard Weber and Misha Malakhov became the first people to travel by foot to the North Pole. They had no resupplies and no outside help. They left from the Ward Hunt ice shelf and it took them eighty-one days to get there. No dogs, no snowmobiles, no airplanes, no resupplies. Of course, they also didn't have randomly interspersed and discouraging messages from a younger and partially psychotic dying brother informing them that their houses had burned to the ground, but still... It took them *eighty-one days* to get there—and only twenty-seven days to get back. Out of context, that fact usually speaks one of two things to me: either they got really lost along the way, or gravity is a lot stronger at the equator and they walked downhill back to Canada. In truth it was so much shorter for Weber and Malakhov to return because, while they travelled there in the middle of the Arctic winter with temperatures cold enough to freeze a seal, they returned during the Arctic spring when they had daylight and even occasional days above zero degrees Celsius.

I, on the other hand, have wacky climate change on my side and can benefit from travelling there *and* across to the other side during the Arctic summer.

The GPS beeps another kilometre at me: 1,454 steps that time. Twenty-three steps too many. Now to aim for 1,455.

I've had a lot of time to think. For example: how and why, exactly, did Santa Claus ever decide to set up base here? Elves never struck me as particularly cold-weather folks. Reindeer, sure, but reindeer would thrive in warmer climates too if you gave them some time to adjust to it. They have reindeer at the Toronto zoo. It's not exactly tropical, no, but come on.

And what was with Santa Claus's insistence on secrecy, anyway? *Why* did he have to be so far away from everyone? Was he afraid people were going to break into his workshop and steal his clothes? Why, on the one hand, does he sneak down chimneys in the middle of the night and have his home in one of the most remote regions of the world and then, on the other hand, sit on his jolly butt in the middle of the Eaton Centre where everyone and their aunt can get their pictures taken with him? I decide that Santa's kind of an idiot and, if I find his home, I'm gonna demand a hell of a lot more than some milk and cookies.

I put one foot in front of the other. Dogsledders have it so much easier. If I had a team of sixteen dogs with me, at least I wouldn't be lonely. I decide that I'm going to get a husky if I ever return back home. A husky and a wife.

Beep. 1,390. Damn. Undershot by a lot. Now for 1,391.

And then, of course, there's Superman. At least with him it made a little bit more sense. I mean, he needed to get away from people once in a while, he needed his Fortress of Solitude to *be* in a place where he could get some solitude. I never understood why he brought Lois Lane there. I mean, yeah, sure, he loves her, he wants to share everything with her. But it's a fortress of *solitude.* It's his secret headquarters and, at the same time, a tribute to his dead parents. It's not a place to bring chicks when you want to impress them. Beside which, you're *Superman.* Is there really no more awesome place to bring a lady than your snow fort in the Arctic?

The icy landscape I've been walking through is not completely uniform. It seems that way most of the time, but I've come to discern slight peaks and valleys. These are rarely of inclines greater than a few metres spread out over four or five kilometres, but they're there. I've started to set up my tent each night in the valleys. Sometimes it means walking an extra klick or two to the subtle bottom, but I find the wind—what very little wind there is in this slowly rotating and frigid, but otherwise largely weather-free, latitude—is noticeably less bothersome.

When the wind whistles by at night it's a high E-flat. I've never heard wind in E-flat before. It's haunting.

Beep. 1,402. Close.

It seems strange to think about, but you're actually moving increasingly slower on Earth's axis the closer you get to the poles. When you're in Ecuador, say, or some other equatorial country, you're travelling 40,000 kilometres every twenty-four hours. That's almost 1,667 kilometres *per hour*. But when you're standing right on the North Pole, you're hardly moving at all, just rotating in one spot once per day. Eight kilometres from the Pole—and oh, how beautiful does that notion sound to me right now—you're moving on the axis about one kilometre per hour. You can crawl faster than that, faster than the whole planet rotates at the higher latitudes.

Beep. 1,390 again. I should aim for that from now on, but no. 1,391. I can do this.

I put one foot in front of the other and then I put that foot in front of the first one, and on it goes for steps and hours and days and weeks. There's nothing to see, there's no one to talk to. The only activity I have to keep me occupied each day is trying to find the caches, something I'm getting remarkably good at. It's like a giant Easter egg hunt across the entirety of the Arctic Circle. Of course, it's a bit more serious than that. If I ever fail to find two in a row, I'm probably not going to have enough energy to make it to a third drop site.

I know I'm being monitored by satellites, through the tracking device in my GPS, but it still feels most of the time like I'm the only person on the planet. The last real evidence I had that other human beings once lived on Earth was that Inuit trading camp. Since then it's been me, occasional postcards from my brother and a harmonica that refuses to operate in sub-zero weather. I can't even see any satellites at night because of the sun. Once in a while a plane will pass by close to the horizon, military and research craft most often, but once in a while a passenger jet. But they fly by so briefly that once they're gone they may as well have never been there at all.

It's still light out constantly, but I can tell that it's slightly later in the year. I can tell that the sun isn't rising quite so high above the horizon as it was at the beginning of this journey. It's not just that I'm farther north, but that the summer is wearing on. One of these days it'll actually dip below the horizon. And then, not too long after that, there might actually be some kind of dimness in the sky, some kind of Arctic twilight. Maybe I'll even get to see the Northern Lights.

I put one foot in front of the other and I think of my dad and my brother, of my mom and of Sandra, if we ever might have had something together, if I didn't screw it all up right before I left, if I had had just one more day to make things right.

FOURTEEN

*T*HE ECONOMY CRASHED WITHIN THREE WEEKS OF Larry's announcement like it had never crashed before. In the past hundred years when there'd been any kind of significant economic downturn, people compared it to the Great Depression. They'd say: This is the worst recession since the Great Depression. This is the highest unemployment, the lowest consumer confidence, the largest dip in the Dow Jones since, and so on. This time they weren't saying that. This time they were using unprecedented superlatives. At least, superlatives they hadn't used *since* the Great Depression.

Biggest Economic Downturn Ever.

Worse than Anything that Came Before.

Worse than the Great Depression.

As with any economic crisis, it was a combination of many things. Increased health care costs for the baby boomers who were all in their final, expensive years of life. A global population contraction that had never been seen before, fewer people of working age simply around to *work*. A lot of technologies that failed to come fruition all at the same time: nanotechnology, zero-gravity mechanization, stem cell research.

A worldwide reliance on renewable resources which, while inexhaustible and cheap as the sun and the wind, didn't employ even one-tenth the number of people as petroleum extraction, refinement and distribution did. Europe dealing with a Little Ice Age. The collapse of both China's *and* India's governments at the same time. And, perhaps worst of all for the world's economy: relatively sound world peace.

Unemployment hit an all-time high in the industrialized world. Blue-chip companies that had weathered every economic storm in history were now in trouble, grasping at each other for support, trying to stay afloat by merging, conglomerating, selling off subsidiaries, withdrawing from previously-developing markets. Whatever it took.

This catastrophe necessarily thrust Larry's health problems to the back pages. Sometimes it would be weeks before I could find a reporter covering him. When, after two months had gone by, Larry was still in the hospital and people were slowly coming to realize that we weren't going to pull out of this crash anytime soon, I found a few articles by minor journalists. And they all said the same thing: that, yes, all of those rich dudes who knew Lawrence Perth expressed their regret at his declining health, at the fact that his cancer had advanced to other parts of his body, that it looked like he would never be able to complete his proposed Arctic journey. They were all heartbroken and expressed their most heartfelt wishes on their own behalf and that of their corporations, but they also expressed a very poorly veiled relief that they would never have to pay up.

Some industrious investigative journalists who had grown tired of the continual coverage of the economy had managed to look into the finances of a number of the corporations *before* the crash and see what, exactly, had spurred them to make such vast commitments to cancer research. It seemed that very few of them could have afforded it and that not a small number of them had taken out insurance policies against the chance that Larry actually *would* be successful in his Arctic crossing. These insurance companies had, of course, bet correctly.

The multinationals were off the hook both legally and morally. Sure, if pressed, some of them would quote a small amount of money that they'd already donated to cancer research in Larry's name, but the journalists strongly hinted that, really, the corporate leaders were relieved that Lawrence Perth was on his deathbed.

At one point I thought it might have been a good idea to try to visit Larry in the hospital. But when I told them my name at the front desk, two large security guards came and, not entirely politely, invited me back out to the street.

A lot of my clients quit seeing me around this time and I didn't have any new ones eager to pursue expensive music therapy sessions. I had enough savings to live off, but I couldn't be anything near lavish. Sandy and I took to having mushroom casserole more often than we were having dinners on the Danforth.

She, on the other hand, was thriving in the downturn. Something about the generally miserable state of the world encouraged people to seek out partnerships and love and she benefited directly from this.

"Why do you think that is?" I asked. We were walking around her neighbourhood on a relatively warm winter evening, just after a snowfall. Kids were out building snowmen and snow forts with each other, interacting like normal, non-socially disabled children do.

"I think people get scared, really," she said. "I think they don't want to be alone when something like this happens to the world. Dating sites usually get huge traffic boosts after terrorist attacks, too."

"Really?"

"It's sad, kinda. Some people only look for love when their way of life is threatened."

"Or their lives," I said, thinking of Larry.

"Yeah."

We went to a playground on the corner where we often found ourselves—one that usually marked the halfway point of our walks. She led me over to the swings, sat down in one and wrapped her rainbow-coloured mittens around the chains.

"How's your brother doing?" she asked.

"You know, I really don't know. Sometimes I can find articles that say he's pretty bad, sometimes they say he's not so bad."

"That's good."

"But all of them say he won't be able to do his walk. They all say he's never going to get out of the hospital."

"Oh."

"All that money, gone. If only he'd done it a year ago. It would already be gone, given to the foundations and research companies before the crash came. We would be that much closer to finding a cure."

"You think there's such a thing?" she asked.

"A cure?"

"Yeah."

I took a deep breath and kicked myself backward. The squeak of the freezing-cold chains made a high A-sharp in the air, echoing through the tiny parkette. "I guess I never thought about it before. I guess I always just...assumed."

"Yeah," she said, swinging gently, side to side. "But that's all right. I think it's a good thing to assume."

As far as the word meant anything, I thought she was perfect. Not like an equation is perfect, not like a logic problem has a perfect answer. Just that she was the perfect fit for me. Or, maybe, we for each other. And it wasn't that she finished my sentences for me or that we had the same taste in music or anything quite so superficial as that. It was that there were parts of me that were missing and parts of her that were missing and that we each had each other's parts. Like, Sandra had the head of a snowman, and I had the base, but we each only had half of the middle ball. I felt confident that we would have a lot of time together, that there was no rush to figure everything out at once, no rush to put all the pieces together.

Which was good, because half an abdomen isn't enough.

I was sad that I could never thank my brother for bringing her into my life.

"He loved you, you know." I had never told her about the time at Larry's place when he exploded at me, chased me through his offices and I had to defenestrate myself from his second-floor into a snowbank. All Sandra knew was that we'd had a falling out, but that it wasn't uncommon for us to have fallings-out. "Larry, I mean."

"How do you know?"

"He told me."

"Huh," she said. And it occurred to me to ask something that I hadn't asked before.

"Did you know?"

"Pardon?"

"Did you know he was in love with you?"

She pushed herself gently, swinging back and forth. "Not exactly," she said. "I mean, I suspected he felt something for me, sure, but then most of my clients are desperately looking for partners and they're not used to women taking an interest. So I suspect that from most of the guys I work with."

"I think, for good reason," I said, and smiled so she knew I meant it genuinely. She knew what I thought of her. Or, anyway, I thought she did.

"What's for dinner?" she asked.

"Your turn to cook," I said.

"I made lunch."

"You didn't make the soup, Campbell's made the soup."

"Yeah, but I even cut myself on the can," she said, and then removed her right-hand mitten to show me a Band-Aid on her thumb. I took her hand and kissed it and she pulled me over to her, our swings on converging angles with each other, and kissed me in the winter evening.

"All right," I whispered and kissed her warm lips again, suddenly far too eager to know every one of this woman's hopes and fears and dreams. "I'll make dinner."

I guess I made noodles or something. By the time we got back to her place, it didn't really matter.

FIFTEEN

I SHOULD MAKE IT TO THE NORTH POLE TODAY.

The North Pole. Me. Alone. Just by walking. My pack and my snow-shoes. My tent and my harmonica and that damnable, constant sun.

The North Pole.

Superman and Santa Claus can both suck it.

It's a beautiful day in the middle of nowhere on the top of the planet.

I'm less than eight kilometres from the Pole, which means I'm travelling slower than a single kilometre per hour around Earth's axis, and for some inexplicable reason I am *craving* ice cream. I don't even particularly like ice cream, so it makes little sense to me. That and the fact that it's minus twenty-three degrees Celsius sort of makes my craving... unusual. But I would give my unburned upright piano—if such a thing still exists in the world—for half a litre of Neapolitan.

Irrationality is something I've been growing used to.

I'm almost seven full degrees north of the magnetic north pole, and it's a good thing I hadn't been relying on a traditional compass, which would now be telling me to head back south.

It's also a good thing I hadn't been relying on the North Star and the constellations either, considering I haven't seen a single sign of them in over a month, since that crazy Cecilia girl at the radar station gave me a brief glimpse at the top of a tower. And even then it was only a reconstruction.

And it's a good thing that Paul McCartney guy didn't catch me trying to kiss his girlfriend. I laugh and think: really, maybe I should have tried a lot harder. There are probably a million things worse than being shot by a jealous lover in the Arctic. But today, I can't think of a single damn one.

Rather than race for the final bit, I take my time. It's been over three weeks since I left land and I'm sure I'm more than halfway to being insane from lack of company and lack of stimulation, but I realize suddenly that I haven't been doing a whole lot of reflection on this long walk to forever. If I'm ever going to do anything once I get back home, if I'm ever going to, say, write a memoir or even, like, a novel or something about this entire thing, I should probably be spending more time looking around, absorbing the damn intolerable, constant, bright, snowy, icy, wavy landscape. Otherwise I'm going to get back and it's going to be a hundred pages of: I took a step, then I took another step, then I took another step. And it was really cold.

So I take my time and I think and, somewhere along those final few kilometres, I make peace in my heart with my little, idiot dying brother. Hell, even if my house *is* burned down somewhere in the world below me, so what? Mom and Dad would both want us to be friends during this final stretch to the top, so, fine. We are.

I should make it to the Pole today, I think, and I look down and see that I'm only four kilometres from it. I can hardly believe it. Although

I've made peace with him, all I can think is that if Larry's watching me somehow from a satellite or something, he must be *pissed*.

I find one of his food boxes two and a half klicks from the Pole and, rather than open it, I decide to carry it. It probably only contains a postcard from Jamaica and a vial of poison or something, but it seems fitting that I open it at the top of the world. I don't waste a lot of energy trying to find the legitimate food cache; I've got enough energy bars to last me through the day and anyway, I'm too excited to eat. It makes little to no sense that I am not utterly exhausted.

I don't know what it's like to be Larry. I don't know what it's like to be in his head and I'm not always convinced, like my mother was, that he simply lives with a difference from other people and not a disability. I can't know that one way or the other. I know that he doesn't understand sarcasm, and I know he's quick to anger. I know he can't read emotions—his own or other people's—and I know he has a hard time talking to women.

I know he fell in love with my ex-girlfriend once.

But what I don't know, truly, about my brother, is if he could have done this. If his condition is such that he fundamentally wouldn't have been able to walk from the bottom of the Arctic Circle to the top of the world. I know he's a little more clumsy than most people, but he gets along okay. In a lot of ways he's smarter than me, but I guess the journey didn't use much of my brain power, just my endurance and patience. Two things that, now that I'm thinking about it, my brother has in staggeringly short supply.

My poor, dying, Iceberger brother.

I miss you.

I take another step, and I take another step. And it's really cold.

So I should make it to the Pole today and then: I look down at my GPS, and I'm there.

Even I, I who have been seeing the same damn landscape for the past eternity, would not have believed how much the North Pole looks *exactly* like ten, or twenty, or a hundred kilometres south of the North Pole.

I laugh and I take my pack off and I drop the food cache and I stand there. And I jump up and down and dance like an idiot.

I stand there at geographic north and I look around me. Somewhere within a few metres of where I'm standing, or perhaps right under my feet, is a spot around which the entire world is spinning. My GPS is not sensitive enough to locate this and, anyway, the spot moves constantly throughout the course of the year due to Chandler's wobble. This wobble makes it very difficult to determine where the North Pole actually *is*, not to mention that it's on ice and not any kind of fixed land mass. Scientists would love it if they could, say, triangulate it between three points on the continents below me. Say, x thousands of metres from some point in Canada, y thousands of metres from some point in Greenland and z thousands of metres from some point in Russia. That's impossible too, though, since the continents themselves are moving constantly each year in relation to each other, at about the rate that fingernails grow. The whole system, relying on three independent points, would be out of whack within six months.

So there's some sort of crazy, internationally agreed upon point called the Geographic North Pole which is, on average, where the actual, physical—or metaphysical, really—point of rotation around which our planet turns is. That same planet on which everyone you've ever known, every single historical figure, all your ancestors back to the dawn of time, were born, lived their lives, and died.

And I'm standing on top of all that stuff.

Oh, if only I had some scotch with me.

And that's when I remember my brother's food cache. I pick it up again and notice that it's not really as light as a feather. I thought it was, but no. It's got some heft to it, some weight.

I sit down on top of the planet and I open it up and the latches give off that familiar, obscene-sounding F that I've grown both accustomed to and pissed off at—but nothing can piss me off now. I hope and I hope for scotch inside, and I lift the lid and see what it is...and I laugh.

How much better than scotch.

How improbably prescient of my little brother.

I lean against my pack and laugh and decide that here, on this spot, is where I'm going to spend the night. I reach into the food cache and pull out one of the wooden spoons he's provided—at least my tongue won't freeze to it. Then I tear open a small container of Butterscotch Ripple and I laugh, and I laugh, and I laugh.

His postcard this time is from Turks and Caicos. It has a picture of a sunny, white sandy beach and I wonder: how could anyone ever find that appealing?

Dear Charles,
   Enjoy.
   Your brother,
   Lawrence

"Thanks, Larry," I say aloud, and then turn to the next tub, which is Rocky Road.

When I've had my fill of ice cream I pack it away carefully beside me. There'll be enough for the morning and, despite the absurdity of it, it really is packed with sugars and proteins and stuff that I'm going to be glad to have.

I lie awake in my tent for a long time that "night," watching the shadows of my tent poles move slowly from one side to the other as Earth rotates in relation to the sun.

It took a while for me to learn how to sleep in the constant light but, as I lie there, I wonder if I'm going to be able to sleep in the dark when I get back home.

When I get back home.

I put my hands behind my head and lie contentedly at the North Pole.

Charles Perth.

If only my dad was alive to see me now. I pull out my harmonica and play the loudest high-C I can manage—it's only good for the single note before it freezes up, but that's all I want it for anyway.

> *Who, alone and beginning in Canada, walked a full radius of the Arctic Circle and stood on the North Pole, taking less than sixty days on this, the first half of his journey?*

I make a promise to the planet then, to all the eight billion people underneath me, while I lie there and turn in one spot at a smooth speed of exactly one rotation per twenty-four hours, that when I get back home, I'm going to find out all of Sandra Miller's fears, and all of her hopes and all of her dreams.

SIXTEEN

*I*T WAS ALMOST SPRINGTIME. LATE WINTER. YOU COULD feel it getting warmer out, the days getting longer. We were about to sit down to dinner on a Wednesday night; she had just come back from yoga.

"You know, it's really too bad," she said.

"What is?"

"That all that money is going toward stimulating the dying auto industry, and building new houses and getting people jobs in the construction sector."

"You would prefer?"

She looked at me as though I hadn't been listening to her for a week. "I would prefer, obviously, that it was going to cancer research."

"Oh."

"I mean, what's the difference, really? If the government donated the money to researchers, rather than providing corporate sector bail-outs? Surely the researchers would hire research assistants, rent laboratory space, buy equipment? That would all stimulate the economy. It's not like scientific research is a black hole that sucks all the money in and doesn't give anything back. Even if they didn't make any headway with the disease, it would have just as much social benefit, or maybe more, than giving money to car makers."

"So what do you propose?"

"Well nothing, really. It's just too bad that your brother's so sick. I've been thinking about him. That he can't do his walk. I'm pretty sure all the plans are there and ready to go."

"Probably."

"And he had enough money to fund himself; and the two hundred billion dollars from the corporations was already pledged, it just depended on him doing it."

"Probably."

"But they got such an easy way to back out since Larry's not *actually* going to do it. They only have to make some token donation to a cancer society in Larry's name and leave the whole thing behind them."

She was quiet then, leaving me to wonder if I was supposed to connect the dots on my own. I went ahead and said it: "You're saying that I should do the walk instead of Larry."

"What?" she said. The look on her face told me she *hadn't* been suggesting that.

"Oh, you're not?"

"No. I hadn't been, no."

"Oh."

So we sat eating quietly and watched the news together. More company bankruptcies. More layoffs. More government stimulation plans that would probably come to nothing.

My lack of clients was finally starting to affect me. If it were possible to find one in this economic climate, I might have thought about looking for a part-time job in some related industry or, at least, something I'd be really good at. Piano tuner. Or give music lessons in my home again.

The commercials came and there was a tourism ad for Cuba—as though people could afford to take trips now. Still, Cuba was cheap. The commercial provided a glimpse of a young couple walking along the beach, holding hands, smiling as the sun got near the horizon. Sandy and I had planned to take a trip at the end of the year, someplace tropical. My lack of income was going to make that difficult.

"But what if I did?" I asked.

"I'm sorry?"

I saw that she had been drifting. She had been working longer hours lately.

"What if I did do it instead of Larry?"

"Walk across the Arctic?"

"Yeah, what if I did it instead of him?"

She smiled sleepily at me and got up off the couch. On her way to the bedroom she gave me a kiss on the forehead. "You're sweet," she said. "I'll be reading in bed."

But what if I *did*?

The next morning I couldn't get the idea out of my head. I decided to go to my brother's house. If he remembered I still had a key, he might have changed the locks. If he didn't, I figured I could find a way in to look around. I told Sandy I was going to my office (she didn't know quite how badly my business was going) and drove through the slush to North York.

It looked like the snow in front of my brother's house hadn't been shovelled all season. I tried the key and was surprised to find that it still worked. It took me a while to find a shovel, but there was an old metal one in a closet in his basement. It was like shovelling snow with a coffee table, but I eventually got the walkway cleared. It was tiring work for me, and I was a fitness freak compared to Larry. I wondered how he managed on his own. Feeling far more tired than was good for me, I sat down on his front steps to catch my breath.

His front lawn, under the snow, looked like a disaster—statues toppled over each other, fountains overflowing with fallen leaves.

I went back into his house, took off my boots and went up to his offices. One of the doors had been shattered down the middle, splinters of wood sticking up from the hall carpet. The pick-axe was lying prone against a wall. I picked it up, amazed at its lightness. For kicks, I took one practice swing at the broken door and punched a hole right through it into the wall behind. Probably the kind of thing Larry might notice, if he ever came back home again. I put the pick-axe back where I found it and went to the other office, the one with all the Arctic plans. It looked the same as the last time I'd seen it.

The rest of the afternoon I spent looking over all the details. Fortunately they were printed out in hard copy. As comfortable as Larry was with computers, I think he trusted them as much as he trusted people—not very much.

The plans called for a 5,200-kilometre journey from the Canadian side of the Arctic Circle, passing right through the North Pole and finishing on the Russian side. Food caches dropped off beforehand to limit the pack weight. A solar-powered GPS to make sure you were headed in the right direction. Otherwise, no other help. No team of dogs, no snowmobile. No airplane or helicopter checking up on you every couple of days. Just one man alone in the Arctic for over three months. Three months of walking.

I've always kept myself in great shape. Ever since I finished university and realized I'd be spending my life as a music therapist. I overcompensated for the inactivity of my job by hitting the gym four times a week—at least my work hours allowed me that kind of time. Still, when was the last time I walked fifty kilometres in a day? I'd done three marathons in my life, but those were on pavement. In a city. In the autumn. Could I do fifty klicks a day, for a hundred days, in the Arctic? I wasn't sure.

It took me hours to go through the detailed itineraries that Larry had made for himself. There was also a very full filing cabinet dedicated solely to the pledges made by the corporations, but I was less concerned about that. If I really was to take my brother's place, I figured I'd be lucky to have them commit even ten percent of what they had initially pledged. There'd certainly be no legal obligation for them to do so; it was Larry's name on the contracts, not mine.

Before I left I took a casual look through his house to make sure everything was fine. There seemed to be a light coat of dust on all the furniture and bookshelves, but otherwise nothing looked amiss. He probably didn't have anyone coming in to check on things. I refrained from going to his refrigerator: he'd have to take care of that for himself when he got back from the hospital...or not.

In his bedroom, on the nightstand, I found a picture I was quite familiar with but hadn't seen in years. It was of me, Larry, Mom and

Dad in Whitehorse, standing in front of the *SS Klondike*, right beside Robert Service Way. Our shadows stretched out behind us and we all looked very happy.

On my way back to my car I walked over to the wrought-iron unicorn and stood it back upright. Unicorns, the narwhals of the land.

During the drive back to my place I thought: how hard could it be? Clearly Larry had thought it through and had concluded—no doubt quite soundly—that he could succeed. I was in ten times better shape than he had been before he went into the hospital. Couldn't I do it too? Fifty kilometres per day. Over snow and ice.

Before I had turned the car into my street I had convinced myself that I could do it. I mean, sure I could. Why not? Why *couldn't* I walk across the Arctic Circle? When I got in, Sandy was still there, on the computer, a cup of hot coffee by her side.

"You were gone a while," she said.

"I guess," I replied. "Hard at work?"

"Not really."

"Wanna go for a walk?"

"Okay," she said.

And so we went for a walk together and while walking I somehow convinced her that I could walk to Russia. After that, it was simply a matter of convincing myself.

But, still, I thought: how hard could it be?

SEVENTEEN

*O*N THE JOURNEY SOUTH TO RUSSIA, I MAKE AN OBSER-
vation: walking to the North Pole is easy. It's walking *away* from
it that's a bitch. Technically, the distance back to the Arctic Circle
on the Russian side is as far as that on the Canadian side. But the
distance to *land* on the Russian side is quite a bit farther. Canada has
a lot more land lying within eighty degrees north latitude than Russia does. In fact, most of Ellesmere Island, where I was last on land,
is north of eighty. The path that my brother set doesn't even call for
me getting to Russia via Severnaya Zemlya, which my GPS tells me
is a group of islands about as far from the Pole as Ellesmere. No, that
would have been indirect. Rather, Larry had planned to walk all the
way across the frozen Laptev Sea to the delta of the Lena River. It
looks rather ridiculous on the GPS to see that I'm going to be walking
across an entire *sea,* but then I realize that I am, technically, walking
right across an entire ocean, so I figure it won't be that weird once I
get to it.

After the Lena River delta, I'm supposed to travel over land to Tiksi
Bay and then the town of Tiksi proper. Tiksi now has a population just

over 5,000 people, though it has had as many as 12,000. It's about ten kilometres or so a-kilter from an exactly straight-line path, but I guess in this case Larry made a concession for political reasons. Tiksi is where the Russian customs delegation is supposed to greet me on their side. It's also, presumably, where the media will be waiting, if anyone back in civilization is still following my story.

I wonder for about one one-hundredth of a second how the economy is doing and twice that long about my house.

And then I keep on walking.

In most books I've read where people travel someplace or go on a journey, the way back home is glossed over as though it were no big deal. Quest completed, everyone survived the journey there, so you can expect that everyone will survive the journey back. Take Tolkien's work, for example. All that solid quest stuff. *The Hobbit.* Its subtitle is even "There and Back Again." But that's misleading. It's not really about Back Again at all. It's about Bilbo's journey to the Lonely Mountain, then that war with all the different armies. Sure, Tolkien gives lip service to the fact that they had some pretty wild adventures on the way back but, since he and Gandalf take the long way, avoiding nefarious mines and murky woods, they don't ever face any *real* danger, and so the journey home can be covered in a page or two.

In real life it's nothing like that at all. Although the North Pole had never been my destination, just a milestone along the way, something about walking south feels like I'm heading home. And the journey home, I'm learning, can be a harrowing ordeal in itself. Even if, or maybe I should say, *especially* if your target destination isn't your home at all but, rather, your father's homeland. A place you haven't visited in over a decade, where the people speak a language different from your own, and the only words you might have in common are "okay," "taxi" and "bikini." And I don't imagine there are gonna be too many Russian fishermen in Tiksi Bay walking around in bikinis.

At least, I hope not.

So, for the past couple of weeks I've been trying not to think about the long walk south. All of my equipment is, surprisingly, still in fully working order. I haven't broken anything. I haven't lost anything either, but maybe that's not too hard when I'm the only thing on the landscape for a thousand kilometres in either direction. If I dropped a nickel up here it would probably be visible from space.

My legs hurt more lately, but I tell myself it's because they've been growing stronger. If I could see myself in the mirror I bet I'd look better than I have since I was a sports-mad teenager. Something about walking three hundred and fifty kilometres every week while carrying a twenty-kilo pack will do that to a guy.

5,373 kilometres.

Each day is the same as the day before. I wake up in the "morning," keeping to no set time limit. (I haven't used the GPS alarm since I saw the polar bear.) I lie in bed for a while, knowing it's the warmest I'm going to be for the rest of the day, and I usually eat an energy bar. I am sick to death of the things but I have to admit that they work; my own personal *lembas* bread. Then I take my time striking my tent and organizing my pack and, if I'd managed to find a food cache the day before that had breakfast in it—usually oatmeal, if I'm lucky—I'll devour that while I walk the first kilometre or so. After that, I walk forty-nine more kilometres and then pitch my tent and go to sleep.

> *What is the distance that Terry Fox ran before cancer forced him to stop?*

I know that about Terry Fox because, during the first weeks of media coverage of my brother, there were a lot of comparisons being made. What Larry was planning was roughly the same distance as Terry Fox ended up doing (though, of course, Fox had planned to go much farther). My brother had to stop before he even got started, but he did manage to raise almost two thousand times as much money as Terry Fox did, adjusted for inflation.

I am extremely glad that, before I left, no one was comparing me to Terry Fox. That would have been far too much pressure.

Still, every single day, I wish I was "merely" travelling across half the width of Canada rather than across the top of the world.

Most days don't change at all and I've given up trying to appreciate them. The sun moves around me constantly, dizzyingly. My eyes have adjusted to the goggles and if I take them off the glare is too bright even when I squint. Snowblindness is pretty vicious; it's what happens when the corneas in your eyes get sunburned. To beat it, the Inuit carve these intimidating-looking goggles out of caribou antlers with two tiny slits in them—a weirdly futuristic look. But they're nothing compared to my goggles. Mine let in zero ultraviolet radiation and only four percent of visible light. The rods and cones in my eyes have grown to compensate for receiving less light than they're used to. It's going to be a painful process getting my regular eyesight back when I return to normal latitudes.

In the meantime I have to protect my goggles with my life. Without them, I'd be as good as blind for a while and then, after the UV sears my corneas, literally blind for the rest of my life.

I keep walking.

The food caches from my brother have become increasingly common and his postcards increasingly threatening. There've been ones from really random places too: Polynesia. Oceania. New Caledonia.

Today's food cache has proven to be particularly hard to locate. When I'm near one I constantly scan the landscape around me. I've become really good at finding two per day, since most of the time they're within a kilometre or so of each other. Usually when I find my brother's first it's easy to find the second one. Lately my brother's have only been containing joke foods, like a couple heads of iceberg lettuce or jars of exotic spices or just fifty packs of bubblegum. Once there was nothing more than a doorknob inside in addition to the snide postcard, and I wondered if he was getting more creative or if the brain cancer was finally starting to affect him. On the days that I find the original food cache first, I don't even bother looking for his. I have no use for doorknobs. I don't need the tropical imagery, and I don't need the aggravation.

Today the GPS leads me to one of my brother's boxes. It's empty except for a postcard from the Bahamas. Specifically, Coco Cay. I'm not sure what a cay is. There are two Caucasian boys on it, sitting on a beach, playing in the sand, laughing together. The message on the reverse side is not encouraging.

Dear Charlie,

I've seen reports that you're on your way back. You're still travelling at the same pace.

From blurry satellite images, you seem to be doing fine.

The doctors tell me I don't have long to live.

Neither do you.

No more food.

Good luck.

Your loving brother,

Larry

EIGHTEEN

"H M," I SAID ALOUD.

"What?" said Sandra. I could tell she had been dozing. We were lying in my bed together, wrapped up in sheets and around each other's bodies, spending an extended Saturday morning doing absolutely nothing.

"Nothing," I said. "Just thinking." And I felt her fall back to sleep.

I was thinking of my first important piano recital. It was when I was moving up to grade nine, and I was only eight at the time. Not an astonishingly gifted child, but still quite a few years ahead of the other students my age. The recital was in the basement of S. Walter Stewart Library, a little community library a few blocks from our house. I'd gone there again afterward, years later when I used to give lessons, to hear some of my own students play. It was then that I became convinced that it's one of the most acoustically perfect soundspaces in the entire city of Toronto.

My parents came, my grandmother too. They brought Larry, even though he was only a kid. He hadn't been diagnosed yet, but everyone knew he was a "distracted" child. That wasn't the best description, really, because sometimes he would focus on something for hours and hours, like he had some kind of Attention Surplus Disorder. Still.

I was as nervous as any eight-year-old before his first major recital. My parents sat in the very front row. The program had me placed third out of six kids. The room was full to capacity. Larry wasn't the only kid there, but he was the only one who genuinely couldn't sit still.

Some kids take to the piano like it's an extension of their bodies. I've seen it over and over through the years. They may not have the greatest sense of rhythm or timing, but their fingers somehow *know* which keys to hit, as though magnetically drawn to the correct ones. It was never like that for me. I knew when I hit a key wrong, but having absolute pitch didn't help me locate the right one. That wasn't instinctive. That took years of practice and sweat and arguments with my piano instructors.

The piece I was playing was Bach's *Sinfonia Number Ten* in G-major. I had been practising it for weeks. I would lie awake in bed at night and repeat the movements of my fingers on the sheets and move my feet on the invisible pedals. I knew the piece by heart and, though I was nervous, I was confident.

When the applause for the second student died down, my instructor got on the stage. My mom, sitting beside me, had her hand firmly gripping both of Larry's. He was swinging his legs wildly in the seats and nodding his head back and forth the way he used to do. "And now we'll hear from Charlie Perth," I heard, and I stood up and went to the stage and scooched the bench in. And I played.

Lying there with Sandra, I tried to remember the playing, what it sounded like, but I couldn't. I could remember the lights, though, the bright lights shining down on me, causing me to squint. I thought that was all right, I didn't need my eyes. I played and I'm pretty sure it was perfect. I was convinced that it was the best thing I had done in my life up to that point.

When I finished I stopped playing and sat there, hands in my lap. I could hear my dad clapping loudly from the front row. I turned to squint through the lights at the audience and I could see him and my grandmother sitting there clapping and smiling, but I saw that Larry was gone. And so was my mom. She wasn't there to see it; she had missed the entire thing.

When she died of breast cancer, in a lot of ways it felt like I was losing my whole family. I couldn't relate to Larry the way you could with normal relatives, and my mom had been a kind of memory vault for everyone who had died before her. Her parents, my aunts and uncles. My dad. She'd have countless stories to tell about my dad, about after he first moved to Toronto and they met at a Legion one night and they had such a hard time communicating sometimes, but that they were always so in love with each other. Well, she never actually said that last part, but you could hear it there, between the lines.

There were still those few things I'd never wrapped up from her will and, lying there, I thought maybe I'd try to get to them before I left to go up north. My mom's house was still for sale and, with the economy the way it was, it looked like it would be for a long time to come. I hadn't been by there since the day the real estate agent put the For Sale sign on the lawn. It was too hard to be there without her.

I didn't resent that our mother had always looked out for Larry first. I mean, I understood that. He was younger and he always needed more help than me, even if he'd never admit it. So I never resented my mom for that. At least, not once I was old enough to understand.

"Hm," I said again, and Sandra stirred in my arms.

"What time is it?" she asked.

There was light streaming in through the window, but I didn't want to turn my head to check the clock. "I dunno."

She stretched and rolled over on her back, cleared her throat. "So. You think you're going to be ready for this in three months' time?" She flopped back into me and I knew she was awake now.

"Yeah," I said distractedly, lost in my own thoughts.

"Charlie, I'm worried. I don't care if you can do seventy kilometres in a day now. There's got to be a lot more to it than that. You can't just get out of bed in the morning one day and decide you're going to walk to the North Pole."

I laughed and squeezed her tight.

"What?"

"Sorry. I was thinking about my folks. And what you just said...I'm pretty sure that's what my dad used to think, back when he lived up north. That he could get out of bed in the winter sometime and walk home to Russia across the frozen ocean."

"But he couldn't have, he would have died. He wasn't Superman. *You're* not Superman. You have to train for this. Do you even know how cold it gets up there?"

"It rarely gets much colder than minus forty degrees Celsius. And for most of the summer it's about minus twenty, sometimes even in the teens."

"'Kay, fine. But you're going to be there for *a hundred days.*"

"I know, Sandy."

"So you're going to do some research? Start eating healthy?"

I sighed. "Yes, I had planned on it."

"Maybe read a few books on Arctic survival?"

"Yes, I plan on doing all of that stuff. And there's a weekend-long Arctic survival course in Ottawa offered by the RCMP that I was planning to take as well."

"Good. That sounds, well...good. I'm glad you've thought this through."

I hadn't really. It was just information I had stolen from Larry's notes.

"How's it going with the Cancer Society?" she asked.

"Pretty good I think." All the donations that had been committed to Larry had been vetted and compiled by professionals at the Canadian Cancer Society. I had been in touch with them and they told me there was no way the corporations would be legally obliged to donate the money even if I succeeded. I was simply not my brother. However, they *were* confident that most of them would pay some kind of percentage, maybe even up to ten percent. So the sum donation might only be a mere $20 billion. I laughed again.

"What?"

"I'm just giddy." Sandra snuggled in closer to me. "That and, you know."

"What?"

"Twenty. Billion. Dollars."

"Yeah," she said. "That's a little ridiculous."

"It's a *lot* ridiculous."

We lay there together and I lost my hand in her hair and thought about what it would be like to be back up north again. Since our dad died I had been up a couple of times, but not for over a decade. I went because I missed it, and even then I hadn't gone *really* far north. I stopped going because it was lonely going without my family.

"I think it's wonderful that you're doing this for him," Sandra said, while her fingers played across my chest like a keyboard.

"For whom?"

"For your brother."

"Oh," I said, surprised that she had ever thought that. "I'm not doing it for Larry."

"You're not?"

"No." And it was true: I wasn't. I wasn't going to walk across the Arctic Circle for my brother. If anything, I was going to do it to *spite* my brother. I supposed there was a remote chance I was doing it for myself; I was at that point in my life where I really wanted to see what I was made of. But, again, not really. I was doing it for someone else. I was going to undertake the greatest thing I'd ever done in my life and, if I succeeded, I was certain that she would be enormously proud of me.

Even though she was no longer around to see it.

NINETEEN

$\mathcal{B}$ARRY WASN'T LYING. I HAVEN'T FOUND A FOOD cache in three days. I know the original ones are around some-where. I know that, if I just stopped walking forward and searched in concentric circles, it would only be a matter of time before I found one. But if I stop walking forward, it'll take me longer to get to land, where there must be food of some sort. Or, at least, trees. I would eat trees at this point.

The locations of food caches simply disappeared from the GPS after the one containing his threat. Since then I've almost always been able to find the original ones, even without guidance. I know that they're still located roughly on the path that's been plotted for me, but, pre-viously, they've been as much as a hundred and fifty metres from it. Sometimes the guys in the planes weren't very accurate. Why would they have needed to be? I would be guided to the caches by satellite.

That was the plan.

I have a feeling there's one around me now. Around where I'm standing and clucking over the GPS. It's been almost exactly a hundred and fifty kilometres since I found the last official food cache quite by accident. Before that it had been two days. I've been living off of protein bars and now the food from the last cache is almost gone. But I know there's one around me somewhere. I can *feel* it.

I get down on my knees and search the ice around me for irregular bumps, anything that stands out against the horizon, anything that might be casting a shadow. Then I get down on my stomach and scan the horizon again, slowly.

Nothing.

I take my pack off and lay it on the snow, walk a little bit away from it and then get nervous. I haven't been more than five metres from my pack in over a month; not since I was safely back on land. I look at it sitting there. My pack. My closest friend and dearest enemy. Some days even more hated than the sun and its damn long, white shadows.

And that gives me an idea.

I'm desperate. I'm hungry. *I need that food,* so I figure I'll try something foolish. I stand back up and slowly, with my eyes closed, peel my goggles off. It feels unnatural to be standing outside and not have their reliable pressure on my face, but I think this is worth a shot. I just have to open my eyes for a second or two, give a quick look around to see if anything is different. With the remaining 96 percent of visible light entering my eyes, surely it'll be easier to see the food cache, if it's anywhere nearby.

All right. I run it through in my mind what I have to do. Then I take a deep breath and force my eyes open and scan half of the horizon, and then I scream.

I fall down onto my knees with my gloves pressed hard to my eyelids, water streaming through my fingers, my eyes itching and burning and the only thing that gives me any comfort at all is telling my poor eyes that I will never, ever open them again.

After the pain subsides a bit, I redact my promise and simply state that I will never, ever open them again outside in the Arctic without my goggles on, and they seem to agree to those terms.

I put the goggles back on and when I'm finally able to see again I remember that I'm hungry and that I'd entirely forgotten the point behind the pain, and I realize it was all for nothing.

I grab my pack and I keep walking. Maybe I'll stumble over the cache if I just keep following the path on the GPS. It's happened often enough. Not often enough to rely upon, but still. Once every couple of weeks or so. Maybe today will be my lucky day.

One day.

After five klicks of painful starvation no food cache has materialized and I realize I'm probably going to have to walk another forty-five before I get a chance to find another one. I consider walking back five kilometres to find the recent one I missed—I'm that hungry. But then my brain overrules my stomach and somehow manages to convince it that forty-five kilometres forward is a *shorter* distance than five kilometres back and my stomach, my stupid, stupid stomach, believes it.

What's the longest Charlie Perth has ever gone without eating?

The truth is, even that's probably an exaggeration. It's more like: there was one time that I skipped lunch because I didn't have change for the vending machine and I was late for a class. Other than that, I really can't remember being hungry before. Not *really* hungry. Not, like, I have been walking about fifty kilometres a day for over eighty days, I am down to a single energy bar and I will seriously soon be rooting through my Arctic pack to see what kind of edible clothing I might have in there. I think the straps around the pick-axe handle might just be made out of leather. Leather is made of cows.

Cows are edible.

I pull out the last postcard I got from Larry, the one from the Bahamas. The children on it look fat and delicious. I'm not sure why I kept it. Maybe I was hoping it would turn out to be a lie.

It hasn't.

I tear off a corner of it and start chewing. Unsurprisingly, it tastes like paper. I make sure I chew it thoroughly into a very fine pulp. Only then do I swallow a part of the Bahamas. One thing I definitely do not need is a bowel problem in the Arctic Circle.

There are a million things I do not need in the Arctic Circle. And a million of them come to mind.

I'm only able to walk thirty kilometres that day and my last energy bar is gone. I decide that water might help ease the hunger. Most of the time I get my hydration when I eat meals. I don't know why, but I've never been the kind of guy who needs to drink much water. I can usually get by with just a glass or two of juice with my meals, even after walking for twenty klicks. Today I stop to make camp and force myself to drink. Water seems terribly unappetizing but I figure it might fill up my stomach, take some of the pain away.

Might keep me from dying.

After hours of unrestful sleep I get up and strike the tent like usual and walk the distance to where the next food cache *should* be. My remaining food consists of half a postcard from the Bahamas, but I'm saving it for an emergency.

I remember seeing a documentary when I was a kid about a colony who got stuck in the north and were going crazy drinking water out of lead vessels and they had to get themselves and all their people down to the south and they couldn't think straight and so they carried with them really irrational things that they couldn't possibly ever need again, like curtain rods.

And I think: maybe the Bahamas is my curtain rod.

After twenty klicks I stop in the appropriate spot and I look around. And I put down my pack and I walk in concentric circles for about an hour and I find nothing and so, out of desperate, irrational hunger, try the experiment of the previous day.

I put down my pack. I stand up as straight as I can. I lift the goggles from my head and I force myself to look around me.

My cry echoes across the empty space of forever and I fall to the ground, head in my hands, tears streaming from my eyes both because my eyes are in pain and, I realize, because I'm crying.

Larry. Don't you understand?

Don't you understand *how damn hungry* I am?

I lie on the ice for a long time, crying in the Arctic, clutching my eyes and my stomach, sobbing like a child. Why did I do all this in the first place? Who's to say that when I even get back to land that the corporations are going to pay up?

Who's going to cure cancer?

I cry and I cry.

"I'm sorry, Mom," I whimper. "I tried."

When I was a kid I used to take our recycling bin in the backyard and fill it up with snow and our mother would come out and put maple syrup on the snow and—

But I can't think straight. I'm too hungry. My eyes hurt too much. And as the pain fades my first coherent thought is that I cannot do that again. I think that I may actually go blind.

My second thought is vague. A memory, but a recent one. From just minutes ago. Before the pain, before the weeping.

My second thought is: what was that I saw?

I feel around in the snow for my goggles and find them. Then I get up off the ground and carefully put them back on, discover that they remain unscratched after all this time.

Carefully, squintingly, I open my eyes again and try to see what I tried to see. I check the foreground and the middle ground and I see nothing. I turn 360 degrees...and I see nothing. Nothing but my pack and the snow and the sun and the horizon in the distance and there's some kind of black bump on the horizon and I wonder: *What the hell is that?*

I reach into my pocket and grab the GPS but even when I turn it up to the finest resolution it doesn't say anything about black dots on the horizon in that direction. It doesn't matter any more. I grab my pack, strap it on and start walking.

A black dot on the horizon sounds edible enough to me.

And I keep walking.

TWENTY

IT WAS ONLY RIGHT THAT I TRY AGAIN TO VISIT LARRY at Princess Margaret and see what he thought of the whole idea. He wouldn't accept my calls or answer my messages and, as far as I knew, I was still not permitted to see him. But I thought if I went to the hospital and asked someone to deliver a message for me, maybe then he'd let me in.

"Hi," I said to the nurse at the reception desk. "I'm Lawrence Perth's brother and I was wondering if someone could tell him for me that I'm going to walk across the Arctic," saying it out loud like that to a stranger suddenly made it seem like, somehow, an out-of-the-ordinary proposition.

The nurse looked at me and picked up a clipboard beside her. "Charles?" she asked.

"Yep."

"You can go ahead. Room 3-D, down-the-hall-take-a-left."

"Oh," I said. "Thanks." It took a few seconds to get my feet to start moving.

Like most people, I'd never liked hospitals. It wasn't, like some said, that it was where *everyone* went to die. It was just that *most* people went there to die. I hoped, when I had to go, that at least it wouldn't be in as impersonal a place as a hospital.

And then I wondered how friendly and accommodating the Arctic Circle was really going to be.

The door to Larry's room was closed and I was tempted to chicken out and leave. I lifted my hand but, before I could knock, the door swung in and out walked a woman wearing *very* inappropriate hospital attire and *far* too much slightly smudged make-up. She brushed past me as she left. I almost gagged on her perfume as I stared after her fishnet stockings and barely-a-skirt.

Inside I saw Larry lying on his back with his hands behind his head. He hadn't noticed me standing in his doorway. I hadn't seen him in months. He was shockingly thin, thinner than I'd ever seen him before, and the flesh hung from his face like old faded curtains. His hair was all gone but I'd seen him bald before so it didn't strike me as particularly unusual. He had a look on his face as though he were trying to solve a very complex chemistry problem. There was a slight red mark on his right cheek. From a distance it looked like lipstick.

I cleared my throat and he reached over and grabbed his glasses from the laptop on the table beside him. When he saw who it was, he didn't seem to think it was unusual that his brother, at whom he had thrown a computer monitor the last time we met, was standing at his hospital room door.

"Come in," he said, and I could hear his voice carrying the same over-enunciation and unnecessary volume that it always had. "Sylvina just left, I think."

"Sylvina?"

"She is a prostitute."

"Um," I said.

"Charles, I am dying from brain cancer. Also the economy is very bad right now. I have a lot of money."

"Okay," I said and went over and sat in the chair next to him. What could I say? What would Mom have wanted me to say? "How are you?"

"My head hurts. Charles, brains don't have nerve endings. You can't feel things in your brain, so you don't usually know when it's in trouble until it's too late. When you get a headache that is not your brain, it is just your skull, the nerves that surround your brain. Charles, my brain hurts. It *hurts*. It is an illusion. I know it can't hurt, but it does. Every day. I can still think, I can still do work, but I am in pain. Also, I am sick all the time. How are you?"

"I'm...I'm all right, I guess, Lar. Is there anything I can get you?"

"No. I have a phone. My computer. My office takes care of everything. I can't remember somehow. Charles, did I ever finish that Inukshuk in my backyard?"

I leaned forward and put my hand on the side of his bed, careful not to touch him. I was tempted to lie in response and I knew that he wouldn't be able to tell if I did. But maybe he'd remember the truth, later, and worry himself to death trying to figure out the discrepancy between what I told him and the memory he had of his backyard. "No, Larry, you didn't. It's still in pieces under the tree."

"Oh. Okay. I thought that maybe—but why are you here today, Charles?"

"I came by to say..." and how else could I say it? "I'm going to walk across the Arctic for you."

"I know," he said. "The Cancer Society has been in touch with me repeatedly." I was taken aback; they hadn't told me they'd been talking to Larry. "They told me you were planning to do it, to get some of the money for research. You will not do it. It is a good thing you came by to visit me today. Don't come again."

"Wait, Larry, I—what do you mean I won't do it?"

"I mean that you won't walk to the Arctic. I refuse. You will get no support and you will fail. Anyway, you don't know how. Charles, I'm dying and you can probably know that I don't care if you die too. If you try to walk across the Arctic Circle, you will."

"I will?"

"You will die. She was mine. I loved her. And you will *not* be the first person to do this. Over my dead body." And then my brother looked around himself, at the bed, at the walls, at the monitors and the antiseptic everything. It was the look he gets when he's trying to figure out if he's made a joke or not. Then the moment passed. "Leave now."

"But Larry, all that money, I mean, come on, for cancer. And all your work. The Society said we'd probably be able to get ten percent of it at least, and if you put in a few words with your friends I'm sure that—"

"*Get out of my room!*" he yelled. "*Get out! Get out! Get out!*" He picked up the phone receiver on the table next to him and threw it at me. I felt a sharp pain on my forehead.

"Larry—"

"*Get out! Get out!*" He leaned to the side of his bed and slammed his palm against his red assistance alarm.

I backed toward the door and fled. Hurrying away, I swore I could hear his dismissive, condescending laugh echoing down the hall.

The next week was difficult. The groups who had been helping Larry organize this thing, from the people coordinating the financial distribution to the company that was going to drop off the food caches and link them up to the Global Positioning System, were all Larry's friends, or in his pocket. None of them would return my calls and if I got through to someone, the person on the phone would ask me to hold and then transfer me to a random collection agency or something else outside of their company. On top of that, it seemed the Russian government was no longer going to cooperate. They used to be behind the idea of assisting some half-Russian half-Canadian rich nerd-boy with making hundreds of rich Western corporations pay billions of dollars to cancer research. Hell, Russians get cancer too. But after Larry had got to them—I'm sure it was Larry—they politely explained they were not comfortable with setting a precedent of someone crossing the frozen Arctic Ocean into Russia. In fact, they insisted, they had *never* been comfortable with that.

"Dammit!" I yelled, after the Russian consulate hung up on me again. "It's all falling apart!"

"Shhh," said Sandy. We were at my place again, surrounded by all of Larry's Arctic maps and equipment and file folders. After his threat at the hospital, I decided to stop by his place and get all the stuff before he thought about changing the locks. "It'll be all right. You'll be able to do this thing. We have to make them see that this is *just* like your brother doing it. That they can afford it. That, in fact, they can't afford *not* to help out."

"But he knows them all, he got to them all. It's this crazy, closely linked, all-powerful cabal of nerds in all the financial positions in all the major corporations in the world. They're not budging. There doesn't seem to be any way around it..." I leaned back in my chair and sighed hopelessly.

"So what do we do?" I asked. "No one's giving us any help, no one wants me to try this, not now, not with the economy in the tank and not after Lawrence Perth has talked to them."

"Well," she said. "I think we have to get them back on our side. We have to make them see that it's in their best interest to help you, to keep to their commitment, perhaps *especially* because it's your brother in the hospital with brain cancer. And it's fatal. You're just trying to do this one last thing for him."

"But I'm not."

"But you *are*."

There was something playing in her eyes that I hadn't seen before. Some kind of mischief. "All right," I said, not quite understanding yet. "Fine. But we still don't have a legal leg to stand on. All the contracts, all the talks, all the commitments are in Larry's name."

"That's okay," she said. "We don't need a legal leg to stand on. We have something better. We have a moral one."

"And how exactly do you think we're going to exercise *that*?" I asked.

"Easy," she said. "We go to the media."

"And how—" She squeezed my hand.

"Don't worry about it," she said, smiling wickedly. "Your brother's not the only one who knows nerds in high places."

TWENTY-ONE

*A*S IT TURNS OUT, BLACK DOTS ON THE HORIZON ARE not edible. Black dots on the horizon are, first of all, a *lot* farther away than they appear at first blinding glance and, second of all, boats.

Specifically, a thirty-metre-long Norwegian fishing vessel that appears to have been stuck in the ice for anything up to fifteen years.

One does not eat fishing vessels, unfortunately.

I'm pissed off and exhausted and my eyes still ache and I'm *starving*.

And I'm all out of Bahamas.

When I get up close I see that it's surrounded by footsteps frozen in the ice. I can't tell if they're fresh or years old. Still, they're the first footprints not my own that I've seen in a month and a half. I can't tell if they're Norwegian or Russian or what, but they look friendly. Friendly and inedible.

I walk around the boat and find a net hanging down on the south side. I take my snowshoes off and start to climb. I realize halfway up that I should probably have called out first, maybe there's someone still onboard and it would be impolite to surprise them. But I am simply far too hungry to worry about naval etiquette as it pertains to boats stuck in the ice in the Arctic Ocean.

It takes what I assume is the last of my strength to throw myself over the side of the boat. I land on my stomach, feeling every hated milligram of my pack follow me to the floor. Rolling over to my side, I half expect to see someone's boots next to my face, some bearded hermit stranded on his boat, but there's no one. I loosen the pack and manage to get to my feet, using the railing for support. It's easier to stand without the pack on and I'm breathing easier.

The boat doesn't smell like much. I've been on fishing vessels before and they usually *reek* of the sea and fish guts. I notice that this one smells like me—then I remember that I really, really need to take a shower.

"Hello?" I call. "*Zdravstvuj?*" I'd try Norwegian, but I don't know any. Before exploring the ship I take a moment to make sure I'm really standing on a ship and that I'm not dead or dreaming or hallucinating from hunger and loneliness. I touch the gunwale. I knock on the railing. I stamp on the floor and hear a reassuring wooden echo. Maybe I'm actually, really and truly, standing on a ship. So, I figure: if this is really a real ship, maybe there's really some real food on it.

I make my way to where I would put the galley if I had designed the boat, somewhere in the bottom, near the back. I find the stairs leading down and notice that it is *extremely* dark down there. I climb down the four steps to the bottom and try to peer down the windowless hallways, but I can't see a thing. I can't even tell where the hallway ends. I'd be able to see a hell of a lot better if I took my goggles off again, but I'm wary and my eyes tell me not to. I walk a few steps down the hall to where it is quite noticeably dimmer and I do it: I take off the goggles and open my eyes.

There is a man standing at the end of the hallway. I shout and jump backward into the light and again I'm blinded. I fall down on my ass on the steps and grip my head with one hand and put out my other in what I hope seems a supplicating gesture—an international request to not to slit my throat.

Somehow he seems to interpret this correctly and I'm still alive as the pain subsides. I shield my eyes from the glare with my gloves, put blinders around my eyes like a horse, then stand up and look back down the hall. The man does the exact same thing and I vow, when I get home, to get rid of every reflective surface in my house. Assuming that it is not, in fact, burned to the ground.

In this case it's the window on a dusty door propped open. I walk over to it, wanting to put my fist through it in embarrassment. But I don't have the strength any more even to lift my hand up to eye level.

I stumble from room to room and there's no one on the ship. It must have been abandoned a long time ago and stripped of all food, every-thing edible. The galley is empty, the bunk room is empty, the map room is empty, the captain's quarters are empty. Even the storage room is empty. Not even a fish carcass. Not even a tiny scrap of fish skin or eye or dried intestine. I go back up to my pack and grab my pick-axe, return to the captain's quarters and start to pulverize the mattress. Despite the sharpness and durability of the pick-axe, in my weak state it takes ten or twelve hits for me finally to puncture the thing. But it is not, in fact, filled with down or feathers, but simple foam. Simple, inedible foam.

How I had been hoping. How I had only wanted something to eat and what I wouldn't give for just a small bowlful of chicken feathers.

Sadly, wearily, I make my way back up to the deck and collapse face-down on the floor. With my goggles off and my eyes closed I reach into my pack for my blanket, wrap it around my head and take a nap.

I awake a few hours later, my feet up on my pack, and I wonder for the ten millionth time what I did it all for and why I didn't bring a satellite phone with me, just in case. Nothing sounds as glorious to me as a single slice of pizza delivered to the boat's address, feathers on it or no.

Why didn't I keep even one can of that canned meat? Why didn't I go back for it?

I lie there, awake, my head wrapped in my blanket, and think of all the things I should have done differently. I feel strange and, if I had the energy, I would sit up in alarm. But I don't have the energy, so I simply lie on the deck of the boat. I lie there in alarm.

I'm confused. I know I'm not thinking clearly but I'm feeling something...something I've forgotten. I have an impulse to take my glove off and feel my forehead for fever, but taking my glove off would mean exposing my hand to the cold and that's never a good idea. Still, it's a bit late in the day to listen to reason, so I peel the glove off and slide it under the blanket and discover that my forehead is indeed hot. Hot and moist. It is most certainly a fever. I reach down the top of my outer gear and through my innerwear to the back of my neck. I'm sweating there, too. In fact, all of a sudden I feel like I'm burning up. I tear the blanket from my head and put the goggles back on and I really do sit up in alarm.

And it's only then, once I'm finally sitting, that I realize what it is I'm feeling. Warmth.

Carefully, I peel my other glove off and touch my palms together. The skin on the outside does not immediately freeze in the air and I'm having a hard time figuring out what's going on in the world. Without much of an idea why, I decide to check the temperature on my GPS and find that it must have broken when I fell down on it. Either that or, improbably, it's plus one degree Celsius outside. That doesn't make any sense to me. It must be busted.

As an experiment I spit on the back of my black glove and sit there, waiting for it to freeze.

I wait and I wait, but my saliva refuses to freeze. I check the GPS again and notice that the time of day has changed but the temperature has not. I check to see where exactly in the world I am and realize I haven't checked in a day and a half, not since before I spotted the ship on the horizon; I'd been rather single-minded since then. It turns out that I'm at the southernmost end of the ice-covered Laptev Sea. According to the GPS, I'm only about ten kilometres away from the shore of the Lena River delta.

Ten kilometres away from being on land again.

This too seems improbable to me, so I get up and lean against the gunwale. If I trusted myself I would stand on top of it, but at this point I feel like I can't trust anything. I peer south and I can't see anything. Nothing different, nothing that I haven't been looking at ever since I first got on the ice over a month ago. I check the GPS again to confirm what it said, but now I see that I'm standing on the wrong side of the ship. I walk over to the south side and I see it. Land.

Where there's land there are sometimes plants. At the very least, sometimes there are insects under the frozen ground. At best, there are quite often land animals.

Edible land animals.

I go back down to the storage room and grab the lightest harpoon I can find. I contemplate leaving my pack behind me but realize that if I don't manage to find something to eat within the first few hours I'll never be able to make it back to the ship and, without my pack, that's me quite dead.

When I get back down to the ground the land has disappeared and I take a good ten minutes checking and re-checking the GPS and my coordinates and the way that I'm facing—everything but the position of the sun in the sky, since it's such an unreliable and untrustworthy bastard—and then I start walking.

It's the longest walk of my life. That is obviously a crazy exaggeration that demeans everything I have accomplished over the past few months but, at the same time, it is entirely true. When I get closer to the shore I notice that the ice under my feet has gotten a lot wetter and a lot more unsteady. I look down and realize that I left my snowshoes behind me and wish I had the energy to curse myself. Instead, I keep walking.

I put one foot in front of the other and then one breaks through the ice and I gasp in surprise—but not from cold, as my outerwear is waterproof. But then I do gasp from cold as it radiates through my clothes like needles and I try to pull my leg out but I can't and then I realize that it is, in fact, touching the bottom.

"To hell with it," I say out loud.

And I keep walking.

At this point land is only about a hundred metres away. Russia never benefited from the warmth of the Gulf Stream; the northern parts of it are warm in the summer, not entirely frozen. Lawrence had expected this, but I wasn't ready for it. The water is shallow from the sediment pouring out of the delta or something but whatever, I break my snowshoe-less feet through the ice, into the water, back up again, back down again, and then, then, then at some point I'm standing on the land.

I get down on my knees and kiss the black rocks of northern Russia and first hear and then, near the deeper waters off the spit of land, see, a living, desperate beached narwhal thrashing, trying to make it back to the ocean. With what must certainly be the last of my strength I lean on my left elbow and I throw the harpoon at it and I kill it.

I quite clearly kill it, there is no question. It's no longer thrashing. I crawl over to it to make sure and, yes: it is dead.

And I start to eat.

TWENTY-TWO

SANDY'S MEDIA PLOY WORKED PERFECTLY. SHE KNEW some very influential nerds at the CBC and CTV and even the BBC. Once they were on board to give coverage of the announcement I was going to make—hair, posture, clothing, cadence and language all orchestrated by my image consultant girlfriend—then the other major media outlets decided to come on board, too. Following my announcement, all the talk shows, all the panel discussions, all the anchors were on my side. And, really, why wouldn't they be? Which TV personality could say their life had never been touched by cancer? Besides, in such trying economic times, isn't it wonderful to see someone bringing back hope to the world? When the government was giving out bailouts that didn't seem to do anything to boost the economy or make things better, why couldn't these rich corporations stick to only *ten percent* of their own promises? I mean, here I was, a guy trying to help his brother; trying to pick up the pieces where he left off, trying to walk where one man no longer could. My poor little brother who had been brave enough to want to walk across the Arctic Circle to raise money for cancer, while he himself was a *two-time* survivor, but was now in the hospital with terminal brain cancer. And he only had about half a year to live. Honestly.

The *entire world* was on our side.

And Sandy pulled off the consultancy of her *life*.

The call-in shows were the most fun to watch. Sandy and I would stay up late—eating nothing but healthy food now, no more mushroom casserole—just to hear some backwoods Albertan call in to Newsworld and try, through simple moral outrage, to hold the corporations accountable.

And after the second week of this, after trying to dodge their responsibilities, after the first corporation caved, we knew we had won. They all fell like dominos and publicly promised to give at least ten percent—some went as high as twenty-five percent—of their original guaranteed donation.

One news anchor was canny enough to know that a public promise from a corporation was worth as much as the paper it was printed on, so he had a long series on his show, bringing on chief financial officers from the multinationals, people with real signing responsibility, most of them—I imagined—friends of my brother, and he would get them to sign new contracts on live television. Contracts in *my name*. His ratings were the best they'd been all year. I think it was just because everyone liked watching these rich losers squirm.

Even the Russians came back on board. I met first with the consul general to Canada, and then the ambassador. They spoke on behalf of their country, saying how proud they would be when a *Russian* crossed from one side of the Arctic Circle to the other, and that they would be happy to welcome me back to their country. Russian television aired an extremely random, half-hour documentary on my family. I managed to catch a bit of it online, though I couldn't understand it. They had pictures of my dad I'd never seen before. School pictures and stuff, from when he was a kid back in Russia.

"He looks just like you," said Sandy, who was watching over my shoulder one night.

And yeah, I thought. He kinda did.

So everything was coming together perfectly. I did my weekend-long training in Ottawa and learned some useful things. One night, a month before I was scheduled to leave, we went out to celebrate at a local bar. People there recognized me and bought me drinks. Sandra, I think, was proud to be by my side and we both got more than a little bit drunk. When we got back to her place I couldn't sleep for all the excitement so I decided to go online to check out some more of the coverage and see what the total promised donations were up to.

Checking my messages, I was surprised to find one from Larry. I hadn't heard from him at all since I'd visited him in the hospital. He had written six simple words: *I will make sure you fail.*

After the wonderful high of the evening, that one discouraging note was enough to bring me crashing down. Was I really up to the task or not? Could I really succeed where my brother wouldn't? His message reinforced all the doubts I had about myself and this entire adventure.

But, more than that, it *really* pissed me off.

I wanted to get back at him. I wanted to make him hurt.

I remembered that Sandra still had a bunch of private information about Larry—his online profile and photos and stuff like that—on her computer. I opened the folder with his name on it and got his password then went to the dating website he used and tried it out. It still worked. Larry never did think to take many security precautions. It was just like the locks on his house.

I went into his profile and deleted all twenty of the photos he had posted there. Professional "candid" ones that Sandra had taken over the course of a few weeks. They made him look friendly, approachable...*normal.*

All deleted.

Then I went into Sandra's own personal photo collection and searched for ones of the two of us. She had a lot. Hundreds, as it turned out. I knew she took photos, and I knew we had been together for a while now, but it never occurred to me how *often* she was asking me to pose with her, just to take something to remember a particular night, walk, dinner together, whatever.

I located twenty of the best. Us laughing together, posing by the lake, holding hands, kissing. I uploaded them all into Larry's profile and then, not really thinking clearly at this point, I changed his password so that he wouldn't be able to get rid of them.

I shut down the computer and went to bed and forgot all about it.

The following four weeks were a blur of activity: checking my equipment ten or twenty times, replacing my snowshoes because I thought I could get a better fit, learning all the ins and outs of the GPS and trying on the strange and unwelcome goggles; no way was I going to need them. There had also been a lot of coordinating with the food-cache drop pilots so that the boxes were all ready to go when I landed.

And I had to say goodbye to Sandy.

"Will you think about me?" she asked.

"I don't know if there's going to be much time for me to think," I said, half-kidding. "I'm gonna be pretty occupied. I haven't even packed a book because I don't think there'll be any time to read. But yes, silly. Of course I'll think about you. I'll think about you constantly."

Everything seemed perfect. Everything fell into place. My little brother was a hell of a planner; all I had to do was follow along.

Sandra was by my side the entire way. The day I left we kissed at the airport and the media took pictures and I thought: this is going to be *great* for her career.

"I'll be here when you get back," was the last thing she said to me.

I held her hand and looked deeply into her eyes and promised her that I'd be okay, and then I walked away down the ramp.

A moment that perfect is only asking to be ruined. Better to walk away from it while it was still a real thing.

Then I got on the plane and flew to the Arctic Circle.

When I landed, I disembarked alone and went to a small Armed Forces base where I didn't feel quite welcome. It was only advantageous in that it was situated *exactly* on the Arctic Circle. An officer showed me to my quarters. I spent the night and the next day meticulously going over my equipment, receiving detailed and unasked-for lectures on Arctic survival from army guys. I didn't appreciate their smugness and sense of superiority and decided that I'd do what I could to avoid the Armed Forces for the rest of the trip.

On my second day there a plane from the south brought with it a note for me from Sandra. I ripped it open eagerly.

The note informed me that Larry was suing her for defamation of character, for destruction of intellectual property, for emotional hardship. He was suing her for everything she had, and I knew that Larry had excellent lawyers. It was, apparently, all because of what I did to his online profile. Sandra was seen to have abused her position of trust. He was dragging her name through the mud, she was never going to be trusted to do consulting again.

She asked me not to phone, not to get in touch, just to do my walk and to forget about her. We'd talk when I finished it all but, as far as she was concerned, we were through.

Because how could I do that to her?

I was stunned. I thought: Wow. How *could* I have done that to her?

I went to my bunk and sat down and had a good, long think and realized that I was very quickly going to get depressed if I kept thinking about it. I bundled up and went back outside. I took the note and my knife and went down to the nearby river. I was going to cut the note into a million pieces and then forget about it. I folded it up small and held the knife against the crease and yanked, then cried out in alarm and dropped the knife to the ground.

I looked at my right hand. I had cut right through the super-strong fabric of my glove, almost into my flesh.

I was going to have to be a hell of a lot more careful than that over the next hundred days, I thought. I picked up the knife and looked for the note, but it was in the water, a few metres away, already drifting north toward the frozen Arctic Ocean.

"All right," I said to myself, trying to put on a good face and forcing Larry and Sandra and all the rest of civilization from my mind. "That's that."

I went back to my bunk and grabbed my pack and decided I was going to start right then. Why put it off any longer? I checked the GPS to make sure it was fully charged, said an official goodbye to the Army guys, and then put one foot in front of the other, enjoying the fact that I was going to have sunlight for twenty-four hours a day. I'd always liked the sun.

I adjusted the straps on my pack and noticed that twenty kilos was really quite light. It hardly felt like anything. I put one foot in front of the other and smiled despite myself.

"This is really gonna be a lot of fun," I said.

TWENTY-THREE

$\mathcal{N}$o one I know can have experienced such miserable joy as eating raw narwhal meat on a desolate rocky shore in the Arctic Circle.

It's not so much that it's delicious as that it is something you can put in your mouth and chew and swallow and then it is inside you. I've finally discovered a use for my razor-sharp knife other than cutting my right-hand glove open. The flesh peels away in ribbons as I slice and it takes some time before I've eaten enough for the reasoning part of my brain to awaken and make me realize what I'm doing. My hands and mouth are covered in warm blood and I drop the knife and stumble over to the shore and vomit my guts out into the Arctic Ocean.

When I'm done I wash my hands and face in the icy water and go back to the whale carcass. It's small for a whale, about the same size as me. I pull the harpoon out of its side and toss it up the beach. It lands on the stones with a loud, insistent D.

The whale's single tusk points south, away from the water. I wonder how long it had been beached on the shore—it had to be less than a day. Probably couldn't find many cracks in the ice for air, or maybe there's a pod of them that live near the never-frozen river delta. At any rate, it's rather far from the water and I figure it never would have made it back off the land anyway before it died and bloated in the sun.

Still. I apologize.

The temperature stays just above zero degrees for the remainder of the day—it's the end of the summer. I decide to spend the night there, so I go into the forest to gather firewood. Forest is an overstatement. None of the trees are higher than my waist and most of them are dead. That's good because they'll burn well, but sad because, well, I miss forests.

I feel revitalized after eating the raw meat. I must have gained a lot of nutrients from the blood before I gave it all back to the ocean. I spend almost an hour gathering sticks and then take my time building the only fire I've had since my first weeks in Canada—back when this all seemed so easy and the worst thing I had to contend with was a little rip in one of my gloves.

The wood burns quickly and I make numerous trips back to the little forest to gather more. Once I have a roaring bed of coals established I go back over to the narwhal, perfectly refrigerated at this temperature, and cut off a long slice of pink flesh. I skewer it on a stick then go back to the fire, pull up a large rock to lean against, stare into the flames and hold my dinner over the coals. I prop my boots right next to the fire and, while I wait for the meat to cook, watch the steam rise from them.

The meat, cooked, tastes like seaweed. It's not the worst thing I've ever eaten. The worst thing I've ever eaten was kiviak: an Inuit delicacy that I tried once in Greenland. They take whole auks, feathers and all, and stuff them into a seal, then bury the thing under rocks for six months until the birds inside putrefy to liquefaction. Then they take the thing out and chow down.

It is only now, sitting on the shore beside the Arctic Ocean, alive after being near starvation for five days, after having walked on empty for almost two-hundred kilometres carrying a twenty-kilo pack over ice, that I can appreciate why someone would ever, *ever* consider that a delicacy.

I eat until I can remember what being full is like and then, on an impulse, I stand up and throw half of the remaining wood on the fire, strip off all of my clothes except the goggles and run down the shoreline. Only once, and then only briefly, do I think: this is stupid.

I launch myself from the shore, jumping as far out onto the ice as I can. I hold one hand to the goggles and plug my nose with the other. I plunge through and bend my knees and waist, cannonball-style, so that when I hit the bottom I'm completely under the water. For half a second I think: wow, I really should—and then I rocket out of the water, through the ice and race back up the rocks to the fire, barely stopping short of throwing myself into the coals. Saltwater is dripping from my face and sizzling in the pit and I'm laughing and shivering and wondering how the hell polar bears can do that all the time. After I'm warm I go to my pack and grab the fresher but no-less-filthy set of inner-wear clothes and layer them on my naked, salty flesh, then stand around the fire until they're completely dry.

I feel exhilarated and successful. I don't want any more meat for now but I go over to the whale and wrap my gloveless hands around its single horn and try to pull it up the shore. It's hard work and I only manage to budge it about half a metre. I figure I'm going to want to eat some of it in the morning and I don't want some strange, unnamed ocean predator to creep up onto the land and drag it off to sea.

I go back to the fire and lean contentedly against my rock. I imagine I'm sitting there with Sandy by my side, around a campfire somewhere in the Algonquin woods. Once the night starts to set in, it gets a bit colder.

I look up from the fire in order to confirm what the hell is going on.

The night: it is setting.

I again run down to the shoreline—fully clothed this time—and look to the northwest at the sun. I'm still wearing the goggles and, with their aid, I can stare right at it. I can see its negative silhouette against the sky. I can see it behind the horizon, the bottom eighth of it cut off from view, slowly lowering down as the black rocks under my feet get dimmer, so perceptibly dimmer. I stand there and watch, disbelieving, and it keeps sinking until almost a quarter of it is below the horizon. It must have started sinking days ago but I was too desperately hungry to notice. And I'd been walking south. And it's later in the year and—

I see a star. Then another. A whole bunch of them peek through the dim twilight.

Look...

I reach into the inside pocket of my coat and pull out my father's harmonica and for once it doesn't freeze after the first note. I go back to sit beside the fire and I play for almost an hour and I realize, finally, that that's it. I finally know what I did this all for: for this.

I don't set up the tent that night even though it drops down to minus twelve. Minus twelve is nothing. At minus twelve I may as well be in the Bahamas, buying postcards to send back home. Instead I lie awake outside in my sleeping bag, quite late into the night just looking at the stars until, sometime around three in the morning, the sun again rises fully above the horizon and blocks them from view. But I know that's all right. I'm on my way home. There are more than enough stars where those came from.

When I wake up the next day it takes me a while to remember where I am, what's going on, why there aren't close tent walls around me and why I'm not shivering. I peel the blanket off my eyes and put my goggles on, crawl out of my sleeping bag and look at the whale carcass down the rocky beach, feeling not as hungry as I expected. I take a piss in the Arctic Ocean and, fully rested, grab my pack and GPS and start walking towards Tiksi.

I can tell that it's going to take me most of two days to get there because, though it's only forty kilometres away, I'm not in a rush anymore. I'll get food in Tiksi and I'll make it to the other side of the Arctic Circle after that, no problem.

As I walk I remember the first time I explained to Sandra what the Arctic Circle *is,* exactly, that it's the point on the planet above which the sun is above the horizon for a full twenty-four hours once per year and below the horizon for twenty-four hours once per year. Anywhere north of that and you could see the sun above the horizon for, say, anywhere up to four or five months at a stretch and vice versa in the winter. When I was explaining it to her I wasn't sure which one would be worse. Now, walking back south, happy and sated and still hating the sun, I'm still not sure.

I consider briefly going back for my snowshoes but decide against it. I'd have to walk back through the ice water twice and it took me all night to get my boots dry. I hope I won't find cause to need the snow-shoes anymore and if I do, well, I figure I'll survive.

Walking toward Tiksi I don't use the GPS so much as follow the river's shoreline. I pull it out once to check the temperature but I notice something strange. It's indicating a food cache drop not far ahead of where I am.

Why would Larry have dropped one out here? It could only be bad news. He must have seen that I made it, that I survived. The media must be reporting my success, the good news, the fact that I made it across the Arctic Ocean and only have a week or two to make it back, down a hastily-built clay road, constructed after the world started to heat up, through northern Russia, until I get to the Circle on this side. What could have happened?

After weighing the possible catastrophes that may have occurred back home I figure I may as well try to find it. What harm could he do me now? For all I know I don't have a home or really any worldly pos-sessions, and the love of my life has left me forever. So even if it's only a box of spices—hell, even if it's just a paper postcard from Mexico—it still might come in handy.

When I find it I first take my pack off and stretch. My brother. What kind of message do you have for me now? What kind of crazy image of palm trees or beaches or coconuts is contained therein? I flip the latches and discover not a postcard from the tropics, but a photograph, a printed photograph, of me and Sandra. We're smiling, sitting beside each other on the swings at the park by her place. I recall it, it was taken one weekend last winter when we went for a walk after dinner and she brought her camera with her.

I flip it over, confused. It's in Sandy's handwriting and says only:

He's dead.
    Come home now, please.
    I love you.
    —S

Inside the cache alongside the photograph is a bottle of scotch, a can of soup and, incredibly, a tin of self-heating mushroom casserole.

TWENTY-FOUR

*W*HEN I FINALLY ARRIVE IN TIKSI IT'S TO A HERO'S
welcome. It seems the whole town had been watching. Hell,
the whole *country* had been watching. It wasn't because Larry, had he
taken the journey instead of me, would have been the first person to
walk across the Arctic Circle from Canada to Russia. Feats of endurance, discovery or sheer accomplishment were no longer recognized
as all that interesting by the general public, who paid more attention to winners of reality television programs. No. From the start, the
entire thing had been about the money, and it is still about the money
when I arrive, safe and sound and drunk on scotch, at the central
square in Tiksi.

Canada and Russia.

The president of the Sakha Republic is waiting there to wish me
well. He's a jolly man with an extremely strong handshake and requires
an interpreter. The customs and immigration agents are there simply for
show. Everyone knows who I am, everyone's happy to see me.

What are the two largest countries in the world?

What two countries share the largest section of land north of sixty-degrees-north latitude?

What two countries did Charles Perth, in less than a hundred days, walk between, across the Arctic Circle?

I spend the night above the best and only tavern in town and, in the morning, start down the long road to Verkhoyansk. It's a simple clay road, but it's better than nothing. All along the way, remote settlers offer to take me in, to feed me, cook me a fillet from their finest reindeer. The media follow me in jeeps and trucks and, occasionally, helicopters. Ten days later I finally get to the outer edge of the Russian Arctic Circle.

I made it. Look Mom, Dad. I made it.

There's a banner stretched across the road saying *Congratulations* in both English and Russian. There is some local and international media. Everyone's asking me what it's like to be done and suddenly it feels like I completed a marathon rather than a hundred days of marathons. I feel like I could keep walking forever, down through Russia, down through Africa, across the water to the Antarctic Circle, back up the world on the other side, back home to Toronto.

Someone hands me an energy drink and offers to take my pack, but I'm reluctant now to remove it. I still have on me everything I started with. Well, everything in addition to a picture of me and some Canadian girl I'm rather fond of.

As soon as I reached civilization all I wanted to do was give Sandra a call, but I figure it's been months since we last saw each other, and I don't think a phone call from Russia is the best way to tell her I'm sorry.

It's weeks before I catch a flight back home. Without exaggeration, some of the most arduous weeks of my life. The Russian media and politicians are determined to drag it out. Now that I'm definitively done, now that I've succeeded, even the multinationals are on my side, clamouring for any and all PR they can get. After all, they had supposedly always wanted to give to cancer research. But now they have to do their damnedest to make sure that the public believes that. The economy is still as bad as when I'd left and they need all the help they can get. A picture of their CEO with me, slayer of rich weasely bureaucrats, was worth a few percentage points on the stock exchange.

Though it's a constant annoyance to have to remove my sunglasses to get photos taken, I know that they want to see my eyes. My poor, over-exposed, painful eyes.

The Russians have me visit Moscow and St. Petersburg and only afterward do they put me on a plane across Russia to Vladivostok for two nights, before finally sending me over the Pacific back home through Vancouver. All along I find the Russians very demanding, imposing themselves on me constantly when most of the time I just want to be alone in my hotel room, quietly thinking. By the end of it I think I understand why Dad left in the first place.

But I'll never understand why he wanted to walk back home.

When I eventually land in Toronto, she's there to meet me.

"I told you I'd be waiting," Sandra says as the flashes go off around us.

Hours and hours and hours later, after I deliver a short statement I had written on the plane, while we're holding hands in the back of a cab, only then does she lean over and whisper: "I'm really sorry about your house."

I chuckle to myself. I suppose I'm surprised that Larry was telling the truth, but I came to peace with that possibility a long time ago. "It's okay," I say and, in saying it, I realize that it is. "So...since I don't have anywhere to stay, how about if we go back to your place?"

When we get there we have a long talk. Well, actually, first we make love. Then we have a *long* talk, lying in bed together, her right hand playing on my chest like a keyboard.

"I'm sorry for what I did to you," I say. It was something that hadn't come up between us yet. I didn't know how to broach it, and I didn't want to re-open any wounds that may have healed in my absence.

"What do you mean?" she asks.

"I mean about changing the pictures on Larry's dating profile. The lawsuit. All that."

She leans up on one elbow. "What are you talking about?"

I can't believe it. "Larry wasn't suing you before he died?"

She shakes her head. I fall back into the edible pillow and laugh and tell her all about it. About the tear in my glove, the radar station, the polar bear, the narwhal, the cold. About being alone in the North Pole and missing her for a hundred lonely days.

"I can't believe you did that *entire freaking journey* thinking I was *mad* at you the whole time!"

"Yeah," I say. "It was a weird kind of motivation I guess."

"What?"

"I mean all I wanted to do was make it back home to make it up to you."

And we cry together and make love again.

The next day over breakfast she explains to me about the replacement food caches, about how each one had cost Larry $10,000 to send and have the data in the GPS transmission recoded.

"Wow," I say. "And what about that last one, the one that you sent to me?"

"Yeah," she says. "That too."

Huh. "Then I'm glad I kept that picture." It's the most expensive love letter I've ever received in my life.

A couple of weeks later, after all the money has been distributed, after the pain in my legs and shoulders and eyes has *finally* gone away, after I've been on every damned talk show in Canada—my consultant constantly by my side, of course—a memorial service is held for Lawrence Perth. The organizers, mainly people from the Canadian Cancer Society who didn't know what a jerk he had been, make me give a speech. I don't say much. I tell them what a thoughtful guy Larry was and that, unlike what many people had been expecting me to do, I did not dedicate my walk to him. Rather, I say, I think what would have made him happier was if (as I'd been telling the interviewers for the past few weeks) I dedicated it to our mother.

And I tell them, you know, that I'm grateful to Larry for everything he had done for people around the world.

The service is a lavish affair, ironic in that it's precisely the kind of thing that Larry would have hated to attend. I find myself almost proud to be there.

Someone I don't know, some stranger in a dark grey suit, comes over and asks me, just after the service, how I really feel about my little brother now that he's gone. I figure he's a journalist and I guess he knows there had always been a bit of friction between the two of us. But I don't quite know how to answer that.

They say the Inuit have a hundred different words for snow. Well, I have a million words to describe the way I feel toward my little brother...but none of them come to me just then.

A few days later it comes to light that Larry had never made a will. I'm not sure why that was, since the doctors had given him plenty of warning that he was going to die. Maybe he never really believed it. He probably always thought that someday he'd get up out of that bed and catch a flight north somewhere.

So all his property—his house, his money, all that stuff—goes to me as his only surviving relative and as his legal guardian. The latter was a position I had never actually exercised, but one that our mom bestowed on me ten or twelve years before. Since I don't have a place to live I move into his for a few months. Then I realize I'm not comfortable there, so I hold a contents sale, then fix the place up and sell it. I only keep two things from his house. One is the little picture from his bedroom of me, him, Dad and Mom, up in Whitehorse by the boat. I place it on the mantle in my new place next to a particular picture of me and Sandra that I'm fond of. My new place is quite familiar. Since it still hadn't sold, I took Mom's old house off the market. The place I grew up in. After I get all my furniture in I realize that it's also a bit too roomy for just me.

Sandra comes over one evening to help me to clean snow from the driveway shortly after I get settled.

"Hey, what do you think if we got a dog? A husky?"

"What?" she asks. "What do you mean 'we'?"

"You heard me." I smile.

She thinks about it. "That would be all right," she says. "What do you wanna call him?"

"I dunno." I really hadn't given it much thought. "What about Victor? Or...Paul McCartney?"

"Paul McCartney? You mean, like the musician?"

I look sternly over my snow shovel at her. "No," I say. "Not like the musician."

"All right. Then how about Victor?"

"All right," I say.

"I'll see you inside. I'm gonna go make some soup."

By the time I'm finished shovelling, the snow is falling again, but I figure that's winter in Toronto. I go to put the shovel in the garage and then walk to the backyard, just for a second, to take a look. I like to see how the snow falls on them in the early evening, how one of them always towers over the other; those two nameless denizens in my mom's—in my—backyard. Well, not nameless really, since I know both of their names. I know that one of them is named Lawrence and that one of them is named Charles. A giant, stolid Inukshuk that I made with a rented forklift and a miniature, wrought-iron unicorn who leans up against it no matter what the weather.

I definitely know both their names. For some reason I'm just never able to tell which is which, no matter how long I look.

ACKNOWLEDGMENTS

I'd like to thank the organizers of the 3-Day Novel Contest who put so much work into it every year, and the participants who support it and make the competition fun. To anyone who's ever thought about writing a novel, it's a great way to get started and I can't recommend it enough. Thanks to my family for their love and support, especially when I'd sequester myself and ignore them each Labour Day weekend. Thanks also to everyone who let me bounce ideas off them prior to the contest, including Melanie, Becky, Charlotte, Matt, Sarah and the gang at Massey Hall. Special thanks to Pat and Charlie Coghlin for letting us use their house (in Perth) for the weekend; it's a wonderful, inspiring place. Huge thanks to Melissa and Barbara from 3-Day for helping me pull this together after it was written, as well as Lesley Cameron who did a great job editing it. Great, huge, special thanks and love to Brittan, Doug and Teresa who did the contest alongside me this past year. I couldn't ask for a better trio of partners, supporters, writing masochists and friends. Thank you, Kate, for loving, supporting and believing in me, for being there when I need you and for giving me space when I need it, even if it means travelling alone to Whitehorse at New Year's to look at the ice fog.

ABOUT THE AUTHOR

Mark Sedore is a professional writer and graduate student living in Toronto. His previous entries to the International 3-Day Novel Contest have won honourable mention and second place. He enjoys writing, dancing and visiting the cold places of the Earth. *Snowmen* is his first published novel.

ABOUT THE INTERNATIONAL 3-DAY NOVEL CONTEST

"A uniquely Canadian contribution to world literature."
—THE *GLOBE AND MAIL*

The 3-Day Novel Contest is a literary tradition that began in a Vancouver pub in 1977, when a handful of restless writers, invoking the spirit of Kerouac, challenged each other to write an entire novel over the coming weekend. The dare became a tradition and today, every Labour Day weekend, writers from all over the world try their hand at this creative marathon. Over the decades, the contest has become its own literary genre and has produced dozens of published novels, thousands of unique first drafts, and countless great ideas.

For more information and for a list of other winning novels published by 3-Day Books, visit us at www.3daynovel.com.